BLIZZARD AND BEGINNINGS

TALES FROM THE FAE COURT - BOOK THREE

HELLUCY HOWE

STARDUST EMPIRE PUBLISHING

IN THE BEGINNING...

This novella originally appeared in the anthology *A Perfectly Paranormal Easter*, released in 2022.

This amazing anthology is well worth a read - apart from Blizzards and Beginnings, there are three other amazing stories to gorge on!

Check it out here:
https://books2read.com/u/3n2oOB

BLIZZARDS AND BEGINNINGS

HELLUCY HOWE

DEDICATION

For my fellow authors, interested family members and all those folk who love fairy tales, as I do.

CHAPTER ONE

LYSSICA

*F*ace pressed to the window, Lady Lyssica Aphiski stared at the soft falling snow, a moue of dismay twisting her mouth. Each new flake drifted on the wind's sigh, before inexorably dropping to freshen the ground's rapidly whitening carpet.

Winter's first snow? Already?

The frosty evidence was undeniable, even though leaves remained on most trees, and Juberd, the first moon of winter, was yet two weeks away.

"Goddess blast it." Lyssica pressed frustrated fingers to the glass – the tips forming claws – as if she could grab fistfuls of the wet stuff and somehow dispose of it. The early seasonal change would play havoc with the Duchy's horticultural plans; she'd have to adapt her timelines, bring some tasks forward and postpone others. Biting her bottom lip, she fought to swallow annoyance at firm evidence of the Cailleach's impatience to launch her season. But would she want to maintain the balance and leave early at winter's end? Lyssica huffed a laugh. Winter's Queen had never been known for half measures, but perhaps she'd entered into an agreement with Modron, the Autumn Goddess.

Swinging back to her mirror, Lyssica thrust more jewelled pins into her chignon. It was as well the Tri-moon apprentices were arriving today, because, if snow continued, travel would become difficult. Speaking of – she needed to hurry, or the apprentices would arrive at the front door before she did, and wouldn't Papan be thrilled about that?

The chignon's upsweep captured her wild mass of ebony hair, although the swathe of emerald above her left temple and swirl of lavender near her right ear were still prominent. If she turned her head, she'd see cobalt streaks which—

The antique Godfather clock in the downstairs antechamber gonged, the reverberations clanging through her revery. *Shite, Lyssica, get a move on!* Snatching up her makeup kit, she flicked it open and grabbed an applicator.

"Tig, could you please bring my mulberry cling-boots from the dressing room?" The words had barely left her lips when Antigony Lyonetti appeared in the mirror's background; her hair slightly dishevelled, but mouth curved with satisfaction, she brandished said footwear, trophy style.

"One step ahead of you, Lady Lyss."

"Excellent." Lyssica swept blush powder across her cheeks, pausing to contemplate the effect. Nodded. The peach was the perfect colour for her. Using a fingertip, she framed her aquamarine eyes with kohl and the lids with glimmering deep purple before wiping her fingers clean with a soft cloth. Smoothing her fitted violet silken shell, she assessed her outfit; the golden accents on the tunic-length garment went a long way to elevate the outfit from stark simplicity. Just below her hips, the tailored violet and gold trousers flowed down her legs to bell slightly around the lower leg and cuff at the ankle. "What do you think, Tig? I'm trying to look like a professional without losing femininity." She twisted this way and that.

"Everyone will fall at your feet, Lady Lyss." Antigony nodded as she proffered the shin-high boots. "And these will be the perfect finishing touch. Your Papan can't fail to be impressed."

Lyssica grimaced. "Let's hope you're right."

Rattling noises had Antigony hurrying to the window. "Carriages coming up the driveway Lady Lyss!"

"Goddess blast it!" Lyssica slid one foot into a boot, tabbing the side clasp shut as she hobbled for the stairway.

"Your cloak, milady!" Antigony chased after her, the indigo-coloured velvet garment held wide. Glancing back, Lyssica was startled by the cloak's resemblance to a storm sweeping in, then the soft folds enveloped her and the gold fastener clicked into place at her throat.

"Thanks, Tig." She reeled down the tower staircase, the cloak billowing. At the bottom, Lyssica clutched the railing with one hand, lifted her stocking clad foot, positioned her boot, fumbled with the buckle and – hissed as it slipped from her grasp.

"Hell's horns!" Closing her eyes, she mentally counted out her frustration ... *One duskit, two bunnies, three squizzles and – everything's fine, so slow the hell down.* Opening her eyes, she discovered Entanglit, the Papillion Estate's major-domo, proffering her errant boot.

A smile stretched her lips. "Thank you, Entanglit." She wobbled to a nearby chair, sat, thrust her foot inside and tabbed it closed. Regaining her feet, she hastened out through the foyer to the wide, wisteria-entwined verandah.

Maman's face lit up. "There you are, Lyssica sweetie. You're looking lovely."

Papan, the almighty Duke Yanvian Aphiski, flicked her a stern glance. "Beginning to think you wouldn't make it. The carriages are close."

Lyssica clenched her teeth. Convincing him to accept her as heir, a position left empty by her brother, DeMaksim, departing on Joint Queendom business, was something she'd had to fight for – and continued to – on a daily basis. Drumming her fingers on the porch railing, she refused to dignify Papan's barb with an answer, but memories flooded in.

Papan's refusal to include a nineteen-year-old Lyssica in the estate management lessons alongside DeMaksim. "You are a Fae-female and a lady. The position is above your ability."

"But I want to learn, Papan."

"You misunderstand me, Lyssica. Young ladies don't have the capability or intelligence. Stay within your limits and enjoy yourself."

The words had stung like darts; sharp stabs flaying her skin, allowing the polluted slime of hurt and anger to seep out. Reacting to the poison, she'd taken his advice and gone on a pleasure-seeking spree. Flirting with anything male, drinking to excess and partying her days away – boring but harmless, until she'd fallen victim to a predator.

She sighed, hating the idea of reliving those memories; afterwards, the only thing to save her from her self-loathing and heartache was her sworn oath to the Goddess Ostara. Completing the promised daily ritual became the light of her life, keeping her afloat in a quagmire of toxic ooze where her companions turned out to be users and abusers and her father thought her nothing but a pretty frippery.

It wasn't really his fault, she knew. The Seelie Fae had been a patriarchal society for thousands of years despite being ruled by a Queen. Stupid really. The Unseelie Fae weren't so ridiculously hidebound. Secretly, Lyssica had always admired their attitude. If you possessed the power or the skill, the Unseelie didn't care if you were female, male, or of some alternate persuasion. If you could do the job, it was win-win and you were in.

But things had recently begun to change and the uniting of the Queendoms under singular joint rule was a sign of new times ahead.

She hoped.

Despite the fact that Seelie and Unseelie were now supposed to be one, the changes went against the traditions of several hundred years and there were those who struggled with the new status quo; and some who openly rebelled.

"This first Tri-moon program is very important." Duke Yanvian's voice brought her back to the moment at hand. Lyssica listened. Kind of. She'd heard it all before. A nearby grime-rose bush was much more interesting. Were the leaves bruised?

He waved a hand. "The level of success we attain will set the tone for the programs of future years."

Well accustomed to her father's love of rambling lectures, Lyssica reached to cup a leaf in her hand and was startled into dropping it when electricity zapped her palm. Mouth agape, she stared at the faint leafy imprint singed into her soft skin, then blew on her hand and shook it briskly.

Papan nodded, rocking back on his heels, as usual, completely oblivious to the fact she wasn't fully listening. "So everything we say and do must be carefully thought out in advance."

She peered at the plant – was there a blue glow overshadowing it? Instinctively, she began humming; leaning over the railing as she sang faintly, aiming her goddess power at the roots of the grime-rose bush. It sizzled, so she crooned a few more words of healing and encouragement.

Papan twisted, hands snapping to hips. "Lyssica! Are you even listening?"

The trembling bush sagged, before her quiet words imbued strength and life back into it. Then it brightened. She turned her head, regarded him coolly. "Absolutely Papan. As always you make perfect sense."

A few feet away, Maman chuckled. "You're always humming and singing. I never quite hear what you're singing about, but the plants seem to love your voice. It's no wonder our Papillion Duchy gardens are admired and envied by visitors."

Lyssica stiffened, flicked her mother an innocent glance. Did Maman suspect something? She dug her nails into her palms. That wouldn't do. "Oh? You think they hear and respond, Maman?" She laughed. "It's not very likely, but wouldn't it be fantastic? I'd adore being able to help them like that." She did adore it. "But really, it's

9

just our marvellous gardening staff and my fancies. When I tell the plants how beautiful they are, surely they understand?"

She didn't admit how much of the gardens' beauty actually was due to her nurturing. Couldn't admit it even if she wanted to; Ostara had enspelled Lyssica's silence for her own protection.

But Lyssica found there were folk who wanted a reason for everything. *'You must have a green thumb!'* Was a comment she'd heard several times, when her thumb had nothing to do with it – the wonderful results were a direct response to the use of her goddess-given power. Her *Unseelie* goddess-given power. In a territory where the worshipped spring deity had always been the Seelie Goddess, Olwen, Lyssica was a handmaiden of Ostara.

Her father's hand clasping her arm jolted her into the moment. "Stop that infernal singing and look sharp; we've a reputation to uphold, Lyssica."

She wrenched her arm free and, holding her father's gaze, pointed. "Those plants aren't thriving in this early cold snap. Last night's snowfall was untimely, and unnatural."

Duke Yanvian beetled his brows. "Maybe Modron, the Autumn Goddess, wanted to leave early, she is female after all. The phrase 'changeable as the weather' is often used to describe the unsettled minds of females; neither easily explained. Early winters are never a good thing for crops and everyone will be in the same predicament. We can't be held accountable for the weather, Lyssica. We'll do the best we can."

Lyssica clasped her fingers together tightly. "Heavy snow three weeks early has nothing to do with the workings of female minds. With what promises to be a harsh winter looming, forage in the forest will diminish quickly and survival for any living being will become difficult."

"Oh, don't worry." Duke Yanvian waved a hand as the first carriage floated to a stop at the base of the colonnaded portico, popped out supporting legs, and settled. The second conveyance drifted to a stop and planted itself close behind. "We'll feed any deer seeking shelter on the estate, as we've always done."

Lyssica bit her lip; she worried for more than the deer, but their argument must wait. Below them, carriage doors opened, their inbuilt steps automatically descending. Shivering, she clutched at the edges of her velvet cloak; her dracon genetics responded to her unconscious prompt and upped her internal furnace until the cold vanished from her system. Smoothing her hands down her tunic, she drew a deep breath. Winter wasn't going to leave and neither were the new arrivals.

The candidates were engaging in the programme of reciprocal sponsorships discussed and approved at the last United Queendom's Summer Council. Selected single adult children of participating families were to spend the three moons of winter as apprentices at other properties. Some larger estates had accepted several apprentices and agreed to send more than one of their offspring elsewhere. It was embraced as a way to extend skills, promote cooperation, encourage friendships and see if any parties located suitable mates or consorts. Lyssica grimaced; a training program yes, but also a marriage market. Now, five Fae-males and one Fae-female stood on the lower steps.

Duchesse Azura entwined her gloved hands. "I hope our girls have arrived at their destinations safely."

Her consort flashed her a smile. "I'm certain they have. You needn't worry so, my dear." His smile faded. "It's a pity Trey refused. I think it would've benefitted him."

The Duchesse tilted her hand, palm upward. "You know he can't process things on short notice. At least he agreed to join next year's program."

Duke Yanvian nodded. "Better than absolute repudiation, which we all know he's capable of."

Their Tri-moon guests climbed the steps, their features becoming easier to pick out. Staring in consternation, Lyssica tuned her parents out. *Is that...? No, surely not.* But it was. In the advancing group were two faces she'd wished never to see again. Lord Perris Momphiday and Lord Venaday Tortrician. The first regarded her with a sly smile and one elevated eyebrow, the second rubbed his hands while grinning hugely.

Shite, bugger, and hell's horns! *I'm going to be sick.* No, no, she wouldn't. She couldn't. Swallowing harshly, she tried to rope in her errant emotions and thoughts. *Should have paid more attention when Papan showed me the lists! At least I'd have been more prepared. Maybe.* She dug fingernails into palms. *Don't look at him.* She turned her attention to the other four Fae-folk. She didn't recognise any of them; their wings were either tightly furled against the snow or tucked under cloaks so she there were no wing markings to help her.

Duke Yanvian spread his hands. "Welcome all!"

Duchesse Azura smiled widely. "You must be chilled. Let's retire to the salon for refreshments. The house is infinitely warmer."

Lyssica forced a smile. "So pleased." *Not.* At least, not to see— She shook her head internally. "Don't worry about your luggage, it will be taken to your rooms."

Cutting ruthlessly across the path of his companions to halt in front of her, Lord Venaday swept Lyssica a bow. "Lady Lyssica! Such a thrill to be in your delightful company again. Perhaps we can play cards as we used to? You remember the 'Swig or Strip' parties, don't you?"

"Oh! I can't say I do." *More than I'd like to.* "Are you sure I was involved? We were all very young back then and these days my time is filled with important tasks." Lyssica forced a smile. "As I'm certain your life is, Lord Venaday. I hope we have all changed and matured."

"Not too much change, I hope," he said, waggling his brows at her before moving to follow her mother.

Left by herself, Lyssica wasn't certain whether to laugh hysterically, hiss with anger, or cry in despair. Of course, she couldn't do any of those until she was safely back in her room and away from — She shuddered then pinched the bridge of her nose. How was she going to go in there and pretend like everything was normal?

Goddess help me, please. A zing shot through her body, electrifying every hair; she was left with the uneasy feeling that her words had been answered.

But what was her answer?

CHAPTER TWO

EMRYN

*E*mryn made a mental note to thank the Duke and Duchesse of Garadenya for sending the coach which drastically shortened his lengthy trip from the Kynthcat domains. Despite the fact his inner Kynthcat preferred to run rather than ride inside a stuffy carriage, even at top speed, it would take more than a week to travel on foot. The comfortable leather seats became more welcome the further they travelled from the heat of the Destrion Changeling Territory to the colder southern lands.

Even so, as they neared their destination, Emryn, awed by the massive trees of the forest lining both sides of the road, pulled the internal carriage cord for the driver to stop the coach. Grabbing his change-bag, he jumped out of the carriage and onto the road, consumed by the urge to explore despite the chill.

"I wish to finish the journey four-pawed, Brandon."

The coach driver wasn't the least bit bothered. "Sure, just continue on down this road. The entrance to the island estate is on the bridge you'll come to in a few leagues. I'll advise the gate guards to look out for you." He waved. "See you at Garadenya, Lord Emryn."

Emryn watched the carriage disappear around the next bend

before he stepped off the road behind some bushes, stripped, stashed his clothing in the bag then tucked it into the crook of a tree branch. Even thus engaged, he was unable to stop staring at the lush beauty of the place. The forest thrilled both sides of him. As a Fae-male, he was awed by the massive wooden trunks with their canopies of branches and leaves, bulbous roots hugging the earth and the decaying litter of many seasons. His changeling animal wanted to get in amongst it all.

'Want to come out and see.'

'In a few moments.' He wandered deeper into the woods, shivering at the unaccustomed cool climate feathering his naked skin, but revelled in the chill for the same reason. It was so different to the hot dryness he was used to and he craned his head, soaking up the forest's peaceful ambience. Finally, regardless of the cold, he lay down to stare meditatively up into the greenery above him.

His dual senses were awash with sensation and each side of him wanted to manage the inundation differently. The change shimmered over them within seconds and Fae-male, Emryn, became a very large wildcat, his blissful awe eclipsed by a cat's curiosity.

'We play!' Kynthcat shushed his prowling paws through the rustling leaves while marvelling at the lack of sandy desert and towering monoliths of their home territory. His entrancement when he discovered an effervescent spring, leaping and burbling until it overflowed into a tinkling creek, had him springing about like a kitten. He stalked the dancing creek cutting through the ancient woods; his paws slipped on stones as he poked at bubbles with a claw.

A squawking bird with bright plumage winged over him. Head high he pranced after it. Too bad it was soon lost to view in the forest – but there was so much to see and scent. His interest was quickly reclaimed by the magic of the deep woods. His playfulness gave way to careful exploration and the training of years took over. As he padded carefully on through the leafy mulch of the treed wilderness, he kept to hard ground to ensure his large paws left little sign of his passage.

Wending around the bole of a forest giant, he leapt over a gnarled root and made for the game trail twisting away through the undergrowth. The stench of a skunweasel assaulted his nostrils and he veered from the path, shaking his head and sneezing. His rich brown mane waved wildly, the braided lengths flopping in front of his beleaguered muzzle as he lifted a paw to bat away the disgusting odour.

"Blech!" The exclamation emerged as a snarling cough. *'Not that way!'* Emryn fully agreed; even though his horns, claws and fangs would make short work of the creature, the varmint's revolting smell would cling for days. It was better not to endure a face to face with such a one. Changing course, he bypassed the trail left by the foul skunweasel, steering clear of its pervading rottenness as he stalked regally between the trees and circled in a different direction to return to the water course.

Senses alert, he lowered his muzzle to the water, tonguing up the chilly liquid; even were he in familiar territory, relaxed vigilance was never a good choice. Concealed by the undergrowth flanking the creek, Kynthcat wove his way downstream towards the Rubiconia River. When the creek met up with the larger waterway, he turned upstream, picking up his pace along the river bank.

Much as he'd enjoyed the day, the urge to rest weary paws got stronger with each step. It had been a long trip and this exploration of the stand of forest on the Unseelie side of the river – *Oops, can't forget it's meant to be called the Northern Provinces now.*

No care. Kynthcat shrugged off the politics – he'd had fun, despite the skunweasel. When the road came into view he was grateful. Taking stock of their surroundings, he soon identified the jagged tree just short of the road where he'd stowed his travel bag.

Morphing from four legs to two, Emryn reached into the crook of the tree for his bag and dropped to the ground to open it. He pulled his neatly folded clothes out and wasted no time donning pants, shirt, jacket and boots. Running fingers through his long hair, he twisted the strands into a queue, tying the length off with the string he'd stashed in a pocket. Lifting his bag, he slipped through the undergrowth and headed for the road.

Setting a brisk pace, it took Emryn little time to reach the bridge. Part way across the first span, he halted, gazing over the stone parapet to the steadily flowing river. The flows and eddies of water had always fascinated him, regardless of whether he was Kynthcat or Fae-male. He'd been thrilled to discover that the site of his apprenticeship-exchange was on an island. Turning reluctantly away he continued his bridge crossing. They were here for three-and-a-half moons, plenty of time to explore the river.

The gated entrance to the Duchy of Garadenya appeared on the right, a break between the two spans of the arching bridge. He strode in through the opening, promising Kynthcat they'd continue across the bridge's second span to the Southern Provinces – the former Seelie lands – to explore, another day.

As expected, he found two guards both tall, blonde and muscled.

Kynthcat bristled. *'We can take them.'*

Emryn sighed. *'We've no need to – we're honoured guests, remember?'*

A thickset, blue-eyed Fae-male blocked their way. "This is the Duchy of Garadenya, a private estate. Please state your purpose." A second, slimmer Fae-male stood at his shoulder, his green eyes wary, sword at the ready. Both wore grey pants, black boots and belted dark green tunics with a 'G' rune on the left breast, their Lepidopter-fae wings tightly furled.

"Good afternoon." Emryn nodded. "I'm expected – Lord Emryn Phengaris, on an extended visit to the Duke and Duchesse of Garadenya. Here's my writ, signed and sealed by both Queens."

After inspecting his paperwork, the heavyset, blue-eyed guard relaxed. "Welcome, my lord. Your baggage has already been delivered. Permit me to escort you to the castle. I'm Naseem."

"Thank you." Emryn smiled. "I'd appreciate it."

"A moment, my lord." Naseem turned to his comrade. "Jarith, I'll escort Lord Phengaris to the keep. Won't be long."

"Aye, captain. Welcome Lord Phengaris." Jarith nodded, sheathing his sword at his hip. "I'll just roust Vingle from his break. He can assist me till you return."

He kept up with the brisk pace set by Naseem as they traversed the tree-lined driveway but slowed as they rounded a bend and the Garadenya fortress came into view. It was impressive.

Built of cream stone, the massive square keep boasted four large, crenelated corner turrets and two smaller ones facing the extensive, cobbled forecourt. The cobblestoned area was surrounded by a variety of lawns and gardens stretching back to the island's forest. The driveway ended where the cobblestones began, so travellers were forced to cross the open forecourt to reach the keep's entry.

Emryn nodded; he recognised a good security measure when he saw one. Centred in the front facing wall, and bracketed by the pair of smaller towers, two arched metal gates waited, one containing a smaller door, which stood ajar. Another pair of guards waited there. One stood inside the keep, backing up the one framed in the opening.

Naseem saluted the first guard and nodded at the second. "Evening Captain Britha, Cyrano. I have with me Lord Emryn Phengaris. He's the apprentice staying for the next three-and-a-bit moons."

"Thank you Naseem." Captain Britha's chestnut hair was multi-braided and beaded then gathered in a loose band at the nape of her neck. Her sleeveless brown jerkin, again marked with the 'G' rune, swept down over black pants and tucked into black boots. Her waist was cinched by a belt from which a few pouches of various sizes hung. She held a spear, not quite relaxed, but neither was it aggressive. Cyrano, dressed similarly, stood rear guard, his longbow holding a loosely nocked arrow. Britha accorded Emryn a short bow then stood aside, gesturing for him to enter. As Emryn watched, the bowman relaxed and eased aside to make room for them.

"Welcome Lord Phengaris. Please come with me. Naseem, please wait here with Cyrano until I return." Naseem saluted and assumed his temporary position.

Emryn walked through the gates. "My thanks, Captain." She turned to lead him through the archway separating the walls of the barbican, a depth of about fifty paces, before they stepped into the courtyard of the outer bailey. As they walked, Captain Britha explained the layout.

"The curtain walls at the front and sides of this courtyard contain rooms for guards and other workers, plus stables for horses." She pointed ahead to the large central tower they were strolling towards. "That is the donjon, the heart of the keep." It was in a wall of buildings on the far side of the outer bailey, directly in line with the main gate. "It houses the great hall and banquet chamber which was the scene for Queen Maerovana's famous birthday feast over a year ago."

Emryn hadn't attended the ball, but senior members of his clan had and they'd described it often and well at full moon gatherings, so he was certain he'd find it familiar. He eyed the Fae-folk working in, and crossing, the Garadenya bailey this way and that.

"The place is a hive of activity."

"Always plenty to do and it's approaching dinner bell time – when the bell sounds, everyone has ten minutes to reach the dining room before the food does."

He looked around. "Are the kitchens and dining hall here too?"

Britha nodded. "The dining hall is in the wall stretching to the right of the donjon, along with storage chambers and the entrance to the dungeons. There's an archway at the end of the storage chambers which takes you through to the inner bailey, a square courtyard with a well. Around the inner bailey are the kitchens and the blacksmith's forge, plus some other work areas."

"And the building stretching to the left from the donjon?"

"The picture gallery, the library, the offices. They front the remaining quarter of the keep, given over to private and guest quarters plus the smaller garden courtyard I mentioned earlier." She pointed as she explained. "Their Graces said they'd await you in the library."

They mounted the steps to the donjon door which opened just before they reached it, revealing a Fae-male who waved them inside.

Captain Britha smiled. "Good evening, Minksalt. May I introduce Lord Emryn Phengaris, our guest for the next three moons? Lord Phengaris, this is our major-domo, Minksalt."

"Greetings Lord Phengaris, welcome to Garadenya." Minksalt bowed. "Thank you Captain Britha."

She turned to Emryn. "I bid you good evening, Lord Phengaris. Minksalt will escort you from here."

Emryn nodded. "My thanks, Captain. I'm sure we'll cross paths again during my stay." She acknowledged him with a smile as she retreated down the steps and strode away. Turning, Emryn met the eyes of the major-domo. "A pleasure to meet you, Minksalt."

"The pleasure is mine, my lord." Minksalt bowed again. "Would you care to freshen up before you meet our Duke and Duchesse? There is a guest refresh-room nearby."

Emryn knew when to take a hint. "Absolutely." He followed Minksalt through the large, stone foyer, noting the tapestries he'd like to inspect better at another time, and into the great hall. To one side of the entrance was a side corridor.

"Through there, my lord. I shall wait for you here."

"Thank you." At the end of the small corridor, Emryn pushed through a doorway into the refresh room. He used the facilities, washed, straightened and brushed down his clothing, checked the state of his hair – still neatly tied in its queue – then returned to where the major-domo waited. "Would you have my pack conveyed to my room please, Minksalt?"

"Certainly, my lord. I'll have it done as soon as I show you to the library." He accepted Emryn's small bag, then led him back to the foyer and into the right-hand passage way. He opened the second door and gestured for Emryn to enter. "Your Graces, Lord Emryn Phengaris has arrived. Lord Emryn, their graces, the Duke and Duchesse of Garadenya."

Moving forward, Emryn bowed, then straightened to inspect his hosts. He was not expecting to see the grey-eyed Fae-male with the shock of crimson, black and silver hair who stepped forward to clasp forearms. "Dario?"

"Great to see you, Emryn." The Fae-male grinned. "Didn't you know whose home you were coming to?"

"No, I hadn't made the connection between Lord Dario Erib-ifax and the Duke of Garadenya." Emryn shook his head, grinning. "When the special invitation from the Queens came to the clan, requesting a beta changeling to take part in the exchange program, we had no idea who was going, or where. The Sand Seers consulted, selected me, and handed over the second message advising the destination, your title and the arrival day, but, that the Duke of Garadenya was you?" His nose wrinkled. "I'd no idea; I was too busy resenting my selection to even think about it."

Dario frowned. "Are you saying you don't really want to be here?"

"Time sands no! And that goes double now I know I'm staying with you." Emryn shook his head. "It's just that my father isn't happy that I'm content being a beta in our clan and he wants to 'upskill' me, then mate me into another clan with a view to becoming a future alpha. I enjoy working with and helping others, but I don't wish to lead. I never have; nor do I wish to have my mating choices dictated by my father. Plus, I confess to some annoyance at being forced to leave home; not all outsiders are comfortable with shapeshifters, but as I said, now I see who my host is, the situation is far more palatable."

Nodding, Dario clapped a companionable hand on Emryn's shoulder. "The time away will give you a chance to clear your head and consider how to deal with your father when you go back. New skills never go astray – the things you'll learn in this program will be just as useful for a beta as an alpha. This apprenticeship will stand you in good stead regardless of where your path takes you."

Emryn tilted his head. "When you put it like that, I can see value in my presence. I appreciate your counsel – thank you." Emryn's eyes strayed over Dario's shoulder to where a gorgeous lady, with green-violet eyes and hair a combination of black and purple, watched them, smiling. "May I have an introduction to your lovely lady?"

Dario swung around. "Emryn Phengaris, meet my darling mate, Zhulija Aphiski Eribifax. Zhu, this is my friend, Emryn Phengaris of the Destrion Kynthcat Changeling Clan."

The duchesse stepped to meet him, ruby mouth smiling, eyes a-sparkle. "Greetings, friend of my mate." She held a hand out.

He bowed over her knuckles. "Duchesse Zhulija, the pleasure is definitely mine."

She laughed. "Just call me Zhu. I'm more comfortable with that. We're so pleased you could come and stay with us, Emryn, and as for the shape shifting? Well, that's no problem, either."

"It's not?"

"Of course not." She waggled her eyebrows. "You must know Dario catches fire when he wants to and I can be rather unusual too. Plus my brother is a shapeshifter, so we've no issues with your alter ego."

Emryn stared. "Your brother is a shapeshifter? Doesn't that mean you and all of your family, are?"

"No."

"Whisky-nectar?" Dario held out a glass. "It's all about genetics. In most of the family it's watered down. My bro-in-law, Mak, is a throwback – the only one who can change fully. So far, anyway."

Accepting the glass, Emryn took a sip. His eyes flowed between Dario and Zhu. "That's unusual. What animal?"

"Dracon."

In the process of taking another mouthful, Emryn spluttered. "What?" His hosts laughed so much they had to hold each other up.

CHAPTER THREE

LYSSICA

The melting snow had become muddy slush, but Lyssica was beyond caring; she needed fresh air and a break from paperwork. Sitting on one of two wooden benches in the mudroom, she kicked off her slippers, replaced them with snow-boots, then nestled into her heavy weather cloak waiting impatiently on a nearby hook. Once outside, the crisp chill of the air prickled her face with invigorating freshness.

Picking her way along the path leading to the stables, she waved to Vinny; judging by his armful of dried growth, the youngster was on fresh straw duty. He grinned and nodded, unable to do more with the handicap of his load, but the happy grin he shared lightened her dull mood.

The chaos of the new arrivals – with two of them unexpected and unwanted, by her – had stolen her ability to concentrate. Lyssica sighed and kicked at a flurry of leaves on the track to the water gardens. Yesterday had been filled with the flurry of her sisters' excited departures and now, of her siblings, only Treymeron was still home. She wasn't surprised he'd said no to an exchange this year, although he'd tentatively agreed to take part next year.

Never disappointed by nature's display, the shallow ponds bedecked with lily pads soothed Lyssica with various colours of blooming lilies. Pleased the plants were looking healthy despite the early fall of snow, she moved slowly along the jade bridge, basking in the weak sunlight even as she checked the plants for the grime-rose's frozen blue blight. Finding nothing of worry in any of the separate ponds, Lyssica continued to traverse the series of ornate bridges linking the gravel paths, until she reached the cottage garden. In front of her rambling roses spread over wide pergolas, framing beds of hollyhock, foxglove, catmint, delphinium, phlox, peonies, cosmos, and other varieties.

Eventually, the sprawling gardens gave way to hedged lawns; beyond the hedges were the trees dividing the gardens from the gravel driveway. Lyssica paused as the sound of yet another carriage arriving reinforced her decision to avoid the drive. Slipping between the trees to the open area between, she spread her wings and flitted to the bluestone gatehouse.

"On your afternoon trip to the forest, Lady Lyssica?" A smiling Fae-woman rose from her seat.

"Good afternoon, Bardia." She flashed the guard a return smile. "Yes I am – could you make a note in the day's records?"

"Sure thing, my Lady. Too bad you'll miss tea with the Countess of Cossidae." Her voice full of sympathy, Bardia reached for a quill. "Take care."

"So that's who just arrived. You're right, I'll be sorry to have missed her." Lyssica waved from the doorway, holding in her shudder until she was out of Bardia's sight. She was so not in the right frame of mind for the gossiping Countess. The postern gate was a smaller side exit, separated from the main driveway gates by two body lengths and a line of shrubbery, which allowed Lyssica to slip out unseen by their visitor or anyone greeting her. Carefully re-latching it, she crossed the road to weave a path between the small plants and bushes bordering the forest.

Walking quickly towards the tree line, she inhaled deeply of the cold, fresh air. Around her large trunks stood straight and tall while, above her head, a plethora of partly bare tree limbs reached for the sky. Her booted feet tramped the leaf strewn ground, damp after the snow, but the mulched thickness of many years prevented the forest floor descending into mud. Her swinging hand touched several limp looking bushes and she paused to direct little bursts of well-being into them. As she progressed, she noticed another shrub with the faint blue glow she'd seen in the garden the previous day. Frowning, she stopped to dowse it with power until the plant regained a healthy appearance, before walking slowly on. The blight she'd seen in the garden yesterday was also in the forest – where had it come from? She'd have to investigate further.

As a familiar clearing came into view, Lyssica sighed and flung her cloak behind her shoulders. Her breath steamed hotly in the frigid air as she inspected Ostara's Circle. Different sized stones sprinkled through it in a roughly elliptic layout, some low enough to sit on, others waist, chest and shoulder high.

When Maman had first brought her and her siblings here, many of the stones had been taller than her. She'd jumped, played and danced between and around them, intensely fascinated, unwilling to leave when her Maman had said it was time. The impression left by the glade had lured her back as soon as she could manage it. Sneaking away a few days later, she'd made her way unerringly back to the stone-filled clearing to explore. Inexplicable joy had filled her as she'd sung and danced.

Surprised when another voice had joined her song, Lyssica discovered a fairy on the topmost stone, singing and dancing along with her. Enchanted, Lyssica had drawn closer to the fairy, even as she continued singing her favourite song about sunshine dawning on a new morning of fresh opportunities.

"It's a beautiful day..." When the song finished, she'd been too awestruck to start another. The gauzy-winged little creature had tilted her head, meeting her gaze fearlessly.

"Hello." Lyssica had whispered, trying not to frighten the fairy. "You shine, just like my song. I'm Lyssica, what's your name?"

The fairy smiled. "Nice to meet you Lyssica. You may call me Ostara. I'm a Spring Fairy."

"Ooh, I love Spring! The flowers are so pretty and the new little animals are adorable. I could cuddle them forever!"

"Hmm. I've got lots of places to look after as the Spring Fairy and I'm tiny – it's hard to reach them all in time for Spring's beginning. I think I need helpers. Do you know where I might find some?"

"Ooh, yes!" Lyssica clapped her hands. "I know I'm little, but I can help you, Ostara Spring Fairy. Please, would you choose me?"

"You'd like to be a handmaiden of the Spring Fairy, Lyssica?" The little creature watched her with huge, serious, sky-blue eyes. "It's a large, forever kind of job – are you sure you want this?"

"Oh yes! I really do! I'll be a wonderful helper. You'll see how good I am when you come back – if you tell me what to do at the start. I'm a very good learner and it'll make me super happy, Ostara. It really will."

"The fairy pursed her lips. "I'm an Unseelie fairy and your family is Seelie – don't you think that's important?"

Little Lyssica's brows knitted. "Why? Maman told me there's been changes happening for years and years, something called you-ni-tee, I think. It means we're all one people." Her lip quivered. "Unless it matters to you, Ostara fairy?"

The gauzy, green and gold beauty laughed softly. "Goddess, no. And if it doesn't bother you, we're fine. Come closer, Lyssica." The Spring Fairy beckoned and Lyssica eased right up to the large rock, thrilling as the delightful being put a hand on her head. "I accept your pledge of service and hereby anoint you as a Handmaiden of Ostara." A tingle flowed through her from the top of her head to the tips of her toes, leaving her giddy with joy.

"Thank you." She beamed at Ostara. "I won't let you down."

"Here, Lyssica." Ostara held out a few tiny berries. "Share these berries with me to seal our bargain."

Those tiny fruits had numbered amongst the most delicious things she'd ever eaten ...

With the memory of the bonding uppermost in her mind, Lyssica executed a couple of simple dance steps, moved into a pirouette as she entered the clearing, then waltzed from one stone to the next until she'd made the full circuit. Even though she'd been too young to understand the full truth of the meeting back then, she certainly knew now.

Ostara, the Spring Fairy, was actually the Unseelie Goddess of Spring, Dawn and Fertility. She was the deity whom the festival of Ostara was centred around – the Unseelie form of the Seelie Goddess Olwen – and Lyssica had become her sacred hand-maiden. The magical berries she'd eaten had enhanced her natural empathy into powerful regenerative skills. With it she could share her gift with any animal or plant, enhance their wellbeing or bring about fertile growth. Despite not truly knowing what she was signing up for, Lyssica had never regretted her choice.

As promised, Ostara returned regularly to teach, showing Lyssica, as her Handmaiden, new aspects of her power and position. She arrived every year with armfuls of blossoms and a basket of painted egg-shaped stones. When she flung the blossoms, they'd somehow take root in the ground and the randomly distributed painted stones were filled with warmth and good luck for the recipients.

It didn't matter what time of year it was to Lyssica, as a Hand-maiden of Ostara she'd promised to look after the welfare of animals and plants and that's what she did. The power wasn't something she could turn on and off, nor did she want to – it was a part of her and she protected the flora and fauna no matter the season. To her it wasn't a job; it was something she loved. It was an additional reason why she'd been eager to help in the running of the Papillion Estate – in her mind, the two positions comple-mented each other perfectly.

Pausing in her dance, Lyssica closed her eyes, raised her face to the sky, and took several enlivening breaths. The fresh air filled her lungs and each time she breathed out, she forced the stale greyness of her upsetting morning out as well.

Opening her eyes on the Goddess Circle, she felt familiar joy reclaim her and spun into a second round of dancing to salute Ostara. From a nearby tree warbled a familiar chorus. Glancing up, Lyssica identified two blush-cheeked chirpers, their pale green plumage framing their peach-coloured faces. A family of wood-bunnies crept out from between the bushes; the parents keeping a strict eye on the three youngsters as they swayed and jumped in time with her dancing.

Further around the clearing, a mother duskit brought out her four kits. Lyssica loved the purple, navy and white creatures with their huge ears, large eyes and bushy tails, but she continued on to complete her circle. Afterwards, moving to sit on one of the middle stones that was a good height for her, Lyssica hummed and waited.

One by one, from different points around the glade, a parade of animals cleared the undergrowth. They approached, chirping, mewing, squeaking or chittering, purring, huffing and whistling, but all wanting a touch from the fingers of Ostara's Handmaiden. For Lyssica, this never got old. She didn't care what sort of animal they were, if they came to her for a blessing, she gave it and, no matter the creature, there'd never been any trouble. Whether predator or prey, the animals seemed to know a visit here was sacrosanct, just as she was.

On other days, she'd wander the forest, or around the estate, touching the trees, plants and flowers, sharing Ostara's magical beneficence as her instincts demanded.

The weak afternoon sun was much lower in the sky when the line of animals dwindled. Lyssica rose and stretched, knowing it was time to return to the estate, clean up for dinner and re-don her heir's mantle. There was a welcome dinner to attend and if she wasn't exactly looking forward to it, at least she no longer hated the idea of having to pretend nothing was wrong to her parents and their six guests. No, seven. Zhu and Dario had taken one program apprentice and they were also coming to dinner. She smiled. Her home still contained Trey; Zhu and her mate, Dario, weren't far away. Her siblings, like her duties to Ostara, always gave her strength and courage.

Perhaps the winter wouldn't be as bad as she thought.

When Lyssica entered the salon where the pre-dinner gathering was scheduled, she was informed all the new arrivals were already in attendance. Thankful for the tradition that saw her enter and be introduced with her parents and brother, she linked her arm with Treymeron's and followed the Duke and Duchesse into the room as Entanglit announced them to the room's occupants.

"This is everything I hate." Trey's voice was the barest mutter. She threw him an encouraging smile just as her father turned to place an arm around her shoulders.

"Why don't you do the honours, Lyssica?" Moving to her other side, Duchesse Azura dropped a kiss on her cheek. Treymeron rolled his eyes as he slid past her in the direction of Zhulija and Dario.

Summoning a smile, Lyssica clapped her hands lightly to gain everyone's attention. "Good evening all. I'm Heir-Lady Lyssica Aphiski. On behalf of my parents, the Duchesse Azura and Duke Yanvian and my brother Lord Treymeron, I welcome you all to the Papillion Duchy. We all wish you a pleasant stay and we plan for your apprenticeship to be successful. If you have any questions, please don't hesitate to ask. If there's anything we don't know, we'll either find out, or direct you to the correct party to assist you with your enquiry. Please feel free to approach us and introduce yourself. Entanglit, our major-domo will announce dinner shortly. Until then, feel free to mingle. Thank you."

The duke's arm tightened briefly around her before his arm fell away. "Well done." His smile was warm. "I couldn't have said anything better, Lyssica. Let's wander and give the new folk the opportunity to approach us." He offered his arm to the Duchesse and when she accepted it, escorted her deeper into the room.

A compliment from her father? Lyssica stared after him in surprise, then shook her head and moved to greet her sister who stood smiling in welcome. Beside Zhulija, Dario and Treymeron chatted with a tall Fae-male who had his back to her. All Lyssica could see was a head of rich brown hair neatly tied in a queue, before Zhulija drew her into a hug and they kissed each other's cheeks.

"Wow Lyss, that was great. Now come and meet our guest – he's an old friend of Dario."

"Of course." Lyssica nodded. "Zhu, you're looking lovely. That lavender shade really suits you."

"Thanks." Zhulija smiled again and tapped her mate's arm. "Introduction time, Dario."

Breaking off his conversation with Treymeron and the unknown, but solid-looking, Fae-male, Dario tugged Zhulija snugly under his arm and grinned at Lyssica. "Good evening Lyss. I thought your welcome was an excellent start to the programme. Allow me to introduce our Tri-moon apprentice, Kynth-lord Emryn Phengaris." He gestured to his companion.

Twisting to face the newcomer, there was a sharp 'snap' as her shoe gave out from under her. Lurching forward, dignity at minus fifteen, she closed her eyes, expecting to face plant onto the hard floor. Instead, she slammed into a firm, unmoving body; solid arms curved supportively around her and brought her to an immediate halt. Flesh instead of stone – a definite improvement, but, oh my. She swallowed. Drew in a quivering breath. And found her olfactory senses inundated with a delightfully musky scent, redolent of the forest after rain had fallen. She re-opened her eyes.

To meet the molten silver gaze of Lord Emryn Phengaris. His glorious high cheekbones framed a blade of a nose, and swept down to firm, sensuous lips over a square chin. Melt in the mouth bronze skin was adorned by dreamy sable brown hair – and then came muscles. She could feel the taut musculature of his body curving, against her, around her – the muscles went for days. And nights. No wonder she'd stopped so suddenly. He was a rock-solid work of art. She swallowed again, dignity forgotten. Would anyone notice if she drooled? Or even, perhaps took a little taste?

CHAPTER FOUR

EMRYN

*A*cting on instinct, Emryn braced his legs and tautened his body as Lady Lyssica cannoned into him. Closing his arms around her was equally instinctive as the breath 'oofed' out of her. Lifting her high against his chest, he cushioned her while she gasped and struggled for breath. He stared into her face, willing her to open her eyes. And then she did, the limpid aquamarine pools gazing dazedly. She blinked and her stare sharpened. He froze.

Paws spread wide, Kynthcat thudded to the front of his mind. *'Oh, yes! This one.'*

Emryn's mind blanked. Intent on a conversation with Dario, he'd paid little attention to the lady while she was speaking. After all, a welcome was a welcome; they didn't change much and he wasn't staying at Papillion, so it was mostly irrelevant. But now the lady and he were up close and personal and ... Lady Lyssica Aphiski's thickly lashed, blue-green eyes captivated him. Gulping, he mapped broad, high cheekbones flanking a pert nose, the whole softened by long wavy hair in swallowtail butterfly colours of ebony, emerald, cobalt, cream and lavender. Below that cute little nose, corners of enticing lips lifted in a weak, but bewitching, smile.

"Good evening Lord Emryn. A pleasure to meet you. I apologise for throwing myself at you."

Emryn's tongue was stuck to the roof of his mouth as if mired in caramel fudge. At last, he got his voice to work. "I think your shoe had a breakdown."

Another uncertain smile from dewy peach lips tantalised him. "Something certainly went inverted mushroom on me."

"Lyssica!" Duchesse Zhulija patted the goddess in his arms. "Are you alright? Does anything hurt? I heard a snapping noise." The hands moved down. "Oh, the heel of your shoe has broken off. I'll just remove both of them so you can stand."

Lyssica continued to meet Emryn's gaze, her breath came and went in faint, choppy pants; the aroma of freshly baked cookies tantalised him.

Kynthcat purred. *'Yum.'* Emryn had no argument.

Zhulija straightened with a shoe in each hand. "There you go, Lyss. Emryn? Can you lower her slowly, just in case of an ankle sprain or something?"

Gaze still locked with hers, Emryn gently let the lady down onto her feet. A slight wince, but Zhulija and Dario now supported her on each side.

"You've sprained an ankle!" Zhulija fussed.

"No, no, I don't ... The floor is cold." She blinked; the snapping of their visual connection drew a slight shudder from Emryn. *'Where'd that come from?'* His attention was riveted on Lyssica.

Still supported by Zhulija and Dario, Lyssica glanced his way again and her mouth curved up. Emryn mastered his scrambling brain enough to smile, trying not to appear obvious as he catalogued more of her.

She stole his breath – ravishingly wrapped in a long-sleeved, ebony dress, the inviting neckline dipping to delicious cleavage between plump breasts. He wanted to pounce; he yearned to lick;

he ached to nip and nibble. Waves of hot and cold swept over him – what was this?

A brush of fur as Kynthcat prowled. Emryn coughed to swallow the faint growl bubbling up his throat; Kynthcat wanted to rub up against her. By fur and claw! She was slaying both halves of him, and if he didn't speak, she'd think him more of a dolt than he already appeared. "Are you certain you're okay?" A suppressed growl imbued his words with a guttural timbre.

She blinked. "I ... I think so."

Dario chuckled. "I was about to say: 'Emryn, meet Lady Lyssica Aphiski' but I think that's redundant."

A new voice intruded on their group. "Lady Lyssica. I trust you're unharmed after that spectacular lunge. A little clumsy of you, what?" His goddess stiffened. He glanced up to see one of the apprentice Fae-males approaching. "Allow me to introduce myself. Lord Perris Momphiday at your service."

Emryn bristled; Kynthcat's claws pricked, wanting to slash the rude upstart.

Lyssica nodded stiffly. "Greetings, Lord Perris." The unpleasant blue-eyed, blonde was followed by a Fae-lady and another four Fae-males.

A very tall, thin, male with ash-blonde hair tied at his nape bowed. "Greetings Lords and Ladies. I'm Tanjil Blastobarm and with me is Lady Kerrigold Helioden. Lady Lyssica, I sincerely hope you've sustained no serious harm."

"Welcome Lady Kerrigold, Lord Tanjil." Emryn catalogued the warm smile Lyssica bestowed on the pair. He memorised the way the smile lit her face; it would be even lovelier if it reached her eyes.

Kynthcat huffed. *Something making our lady uncomfortable.*

Lady Kerrigold clasped one of Lyssica's hands in hers. "Do you need to sit down, Lady Lyssica? That was almost a disaster if not for the quick thinking of Lord Emryn."

Lyssica's smile trembled. "Perhaps ..."

A snarky male voice drowned Lyssica out:

"She tripped across the ballroom floor
Her trip was quite fantastic
She heard a pop
But could not stop
She's wonderfully enthusiastic!"

The bad poetry-spouting Fae-male spread his arms, looking around and bowing as if expecting applause before he turned back to her. "Hello Lyssica."

Emryn disliked the russet-haired, brown-eyed smirker on sight, but he gave Lyssica credit for maintaining a smile, even if it was strained and flat. Who was this tactless swine?

"Venaday Tortrician! It's been a long time." Lyssica glanced from Lord Tortrician to the last two apprentices without extending him a welcome. Emryn bit his lip against a chuckle.

Kynthcat huffed again. *'She no like him.'* He sprawled with his head on his paws. *'This very entertaining.'*

"Melkaz Eriocraan and Roland Arrelgyre! How good of you both to join us." She clasped her hands and nodded. Emryn's superior olfactory sense enabled him to identify her polite insincerity; she wasn't keen on the second of the two Fae-males either. But she remained professional.

"Lady Kerrigold, Fae-lords, meet the Duke and Duchesse of Garadenya, namely my sister Zhulija and her true-mate Dario Eribifax, plus their apprentice, Lord Emryn Phengaris."

Duchesse Azura bustled up. "Oh dear, and to think I was in the dining room when you needed my help." She squeezed Lyssica's arm. "Come Lyssica, let's inspect that ankle and replace your footwear before dinner." Her gaze swept over the gathering. "I'm certain you all have plenty to discuss while Zhulija and I attend to Lyssica's comfort."

Flashing another smile, Lyssica allowed herself to be assisted from the room.

'Go too!' Kynthcat paced inside him.

'No.' Emryn coughed into his hand, covering his growl of refusal. "How interesting." He joined the small talk, commenting

on someone's trip details and ignored Kynthcat's subvocal
grumbling.

Both he and Kynthcat jolted in recognition the moment the
absent trio of Aphiski ladies returned to the room, Lyssica limping
slightly.

'*She in pain.*'

'*Not our problem.*' But Emryn sagged with relief as much as she
did when the doors to the dining room opened to reveal Entanglit.

"Dinner is served, Ladies and Lords."

Emryn was interested to see a round dining table, rather than the
usual long rectangle.

Standing in the doorway, Duke Yanvian cleared his throat. "We
hope everyone will forgive the informality, but as most of us will
be eating together daily for the next few moons, we thought we'd
start as we mean to continue. Please find your place and know that
it will remain the same for the duration of your visit." Moving
forward, the duke held a chair for his consort, then seated himself
beside her.

Emryn took note of the seating arrangements – Duke Yanvian
and Duchesse Azura were in ladder-backed, carver-style dining
chairs, while everyone else was spread equidistant around the
table in matching armless chairs. Lyssica sat to her father's right
with Lord Perris next to her, followed by Lady Kerrigold, Lord
Treymeron, Lord Roland, himself, Zhulija, Dario, Lord Venaday,
Lord Melkaz and Lord Tanjil, then back to Duchesse Azura.

The round table meant Emryn could see his table companions
easily, only needing to turn his head for those either side. As was
expected in polite circles, he alternated between chatting with
Zhulija and Lord Roland, despite the difficulty of keeping his gaze
from Lyssica. If she caught him, he smiled, but otherwise he
glanced away, not wanting to be caught staring. Even though he
was. An unsettled Kynthcat paced within.

He savoured cream of watercress soup, which turned out to be the first of four courses. The soup was followed by a main of herb and vegetable salad with fish, a dessert of honey cheesecake and a final remove of lavender shortbread with candied fruits. It was delicious, even if the 'meat' was fish. Knowing most of the Fae were vegetarians, Emryn resigned himself to hunting to appease Kynthcat for the duration of their visit.

Zhulija turned his way. "Everything satisfactory?"

"Yes, thank you. A lovely meal." He paused. "Did I see Dario swap your name card with his, earlier?"

She chuckled. "Yes, I don't think he wanted me sitting next to Lord Venaday."

Emryn's mouth twitched. "I'm certain you can hold your own in most situations, Zhu."

Her eyes twinkled. "More than most, but I'm humouring him. It has its rewards."

He laughed as a low-voiced comment from Dario claimed Zhulija's attention. He picked up his glass of rosehip wine just as Lord Roland cleared his throat. "Have far to come, Lord Emryn?"

"Yes." Emryn played with the stem of his glass. "I'm glad last seven-day's snow melted before we all made the trip."

Roland swallowed some shortbread. "Absolutely. At least we'll have a comfortable winter." He flicked Emryn a look. "Although, Garadenya is an old stone fortress, so you mightn't be as warm."

"I've no complaints." Emryn met his gaze. "You've been there?"

"Yes." Roland fingered a crumb. "For Queen Maerovana's birthday ball last year when Duke Dario and Duchesse Zhulija completed their true-mating. You weren't in attendance?"

Emryn shook his head. "A representative of my clan was invited, of course, but it wasn't me, unfortunately. It would've been fun."

Roland snorted. "Some of it was fun, but we were forced to rub shoulders with all sorts of lowlife Unseelie creatures. Lowered the tone somewhat."

"Is that so?" Emryn knew there were Lepidopter-fae who

considered themselves the top of the Fae food chain. Looked like Lord Roland Arrelgyre was one of them. "Was there trouble?"

"Oh, it wasn't that." Roland shrugged. "Their Majesty's guards kept everyone in line – it's just that the creatures were *there*, mingling with those of us more well-bred."

Emryn cocked his head. "More well-bred? How do you define that? By district?"

"District?" Roland popped another piece of shortbread into his mouth, chewed and swallowed as he considered Emryn through narrowed eyes. "Are you talking Seelie or Unseelie? North or South of the Rubiconia River? Summer or Winter Court?"

"No. Are you?"

Roland curled his lip. "Of course not. I was referring to Fae-folk who turn into unnatural beings."

"Are not all Fae-folk unnatural beings?"

"You fail to understand, Lord Emryn." Roland glared. "We Lepi-dopter-fae are natural beings who remain ourselves no matter what. We wield magic. The unnatural Fae are those who become something other. They don't wield magic. They *are* magic."

"Ah, you refer to shape-changing Fae." Emryn's voice was a growl and he coughed to conceal the sound. "Now I understand."

Entanglit appeared at their shoulders. "Can I offer you more wine, my lords?"

Emryn shook his head. "Thank you, but could I have water instead, Entanglit?"

"Certainly, your lordship. I'll bring that momentarily." He refilled the wine glass Roland peremptorily tapped, before backing away.

"I've been trying to classify your colouring." Roland's head tilted. "Most of us sport our Lepidopter colours in our hair and wings. My family is from the Argyresthia moth, which birth in shades of bronze and cream, but your hair is simply brown and I haven't seen any wings. What type of Lepidopter do the Phen-garis Clan hark back to, Lord Emryn? Are you an unusual type who can conceal their wings beneath clothing?" Roland sipped from his refreshed wine glass, his eyes sharply focused on Emryn.

"We don't have a connection to any Lepidopter Clan and you haven't seen any wings because there aren't any." Emryn looked Lord Roland Arrelgyre full in the face. "The Phengaris Clan are shapeshifters – we're some of those 'unnatural Fae' you referred to."

A tide of red swept up Roland's face. Combined with his upraised eyebrows, and the peaked quiff of his hair, Emryn was reminded of a startled beetroot.

"Your water, Lord Emryn." Entanglit returned to place a crystal glass beside Emryn's hand.

"Thank you, Entanglit." Emryn grasped the glass and raised it to his lips.

Roland's mouth opened, then closed again. His words, when they came, sounded strangled. "You – you're joking, aren't you?"

"No, I'm completely serious."

Lord Roland eased back in his chair, watching Emryn as if he were a bug.

"You'd better have a bath later, Roland." Emryn gestured between them. "Wouldn't want you to harbour any ill-bred, unnatural contaminants, would we?"

Roland's eyes narrowed. "How did a creature like you come to be in this exchange program? Are the Duke and Duchesse of Garadenya aware of this?"

"Of course, they are." Emryn shrugged. "I was invited, like everyone else."

Kynthcat paced in a swirl of indignation. *We eat this oaf!*

You know we can't. Anyway, he'd probably taste disgusting.

"You must have stolen the invitation! I can't believe the Queens would have approved—"

Emryn yawned. "But they did, Roland, they did."

"This is an outrage!" Although, their interaction had already become a focus to those nearby, Roland's shout drew everyone's attention.

Duchesse Azura's eyebrows elevated. "May I ask what the problem is, Lord Roland?"

"This … this … creature!" Roland pointed at Emryn, who calmly drank some water. "He's here under false pretences. He's not Lepidopter Fae, he's a low-bred shape-changer!"

"I beg your pardon." Emryn looked down his nose at Roland. "But you're quite wrong. My family has an excellent pedigree." On the other side of Roland, Treymeron Aphiski choked, then coughed into his hand.

Duke Yanvian looked to his son-in-law. "Dario? Lord Emryn is your guest – what say you?"

Dario sighed. "Lord Emryn has a legitimate invitation. He is a friend I have known for years and we have no issue with his abilities."

"No issue?" Roland trembled with anger. "How can you possibly welcome a shape-changer?"

"Lord Roland." Duchesse Azura's voice was cold. "Before you say one more word, I should like to advise you that your bigotry is unwelcome here."

Roland gaped, then recovered. "But you are Lepidopter-fae!"

"So we are." Duchesse Azura nodded. "A Lepidopter-fae family who also has shape-shifters in the bloodlines – as do many of the other Lepidopter-fae families and clans."

"You must be mistaken, Duchesse!" Roland shook his head. "Why would anyone breed with such creatures?"

Duke Yanvian rose swiftly. "Lord Roland! My mate warned you that bigotry is undesired, yet you persist. I regret to inform you that you've outstayed your invite. You may sleep here tonight, but in the morning you will leave."

Roland blanched. "You're throwing me out?"

"I am." The Duke of Papillion's stare was icy. "You'll also justify yourself to both Queen Dianathke and Queen Maerovana."

Red with rage, Lord Roland Arrelgyre flung the contents of his wineglass at Emryn. Beside Emryn, Zhulija hissed and flung up a hand – the liquid halted in mid-air, each droplet a perfect, light-reflecting ruby. Fisting her hand, she released her fingers in a forceful flicking motion. The wine reversed course to splatter Roland in the face, before dripping from his chin onto his clothes.

"You … you …"

"Shut up and leave." Zhulija made another gesture, and to the astonishment of all the guests, a cloud of plates, glasses, cutlery and scraps of food rose to hover around her. "Go before you end up wearing all of this."

Eyes bugging, Roland fled.

Fur fluffed inside Emryn as Kynthcat chuffed: *'One down.'*

Emryn concealed a smile behind his crystal tumbler. *'And we didn't have to eat him after all. Bonus!'*

CHAPTER FIVE

LYSSICA

*A*fter breakfast the following morning, the five apprentices joined Lyssica in the foyer for the proposed orientation tour of the estate. She cleared her throat. "If nobody objects, we'll dispense with titles and move to first names." She was pleased to see nods of agreement.

Kerrigold smiled. "All the lord and lady-ing does become a tangle."

"Indeed it does." Lyssica clasped her hands. "Alright, Maman showed you around the manor last evening and Papan will talk about duties with each of you after luncheon. This morning, we'll flit around the grounds to acquaint everyone with the lay of the land." She smiled. "Let's start from the forecourt."

Limping slightly, she preceded the group out through the main doors, waiting at the top of the steps for them to regroup.

"Good morning!" The call had her shading her eyes to check the driveway. She waved at Dario and Emryn walking briskly towards them, finding it no hardship to keep her eyes fixed on the very handsome shapeshifter accompanying her brother-in-law.

"Back so soon, gentlemen?"

Dario grinned. "Emryn and I were up at the first blush of dawn.

42

We've already been around the island and now have business with Yanvian – you touring the estate?"

Lyssica nodded. "We are."

Emryn cleared his throat. "How's your ankle, Lady Lyssica? Are you up to the activity, physically speaking?"

She laughed. "Not if we had to walk, so we'll be flying."

"Oh, of course." He shook his head. "Being wingless, flying isn't my first thought, but I'll be sorry to miss the event – Zhu has been talking about your beautiful gardens since I arrived." Emryn's pale eyes glowed. She had first thought them silver, but maybe they were a frosty pearl? "Perhaps I could join you all later, Lady Lyssica?"

"Please call me Lyssica." She smiled again. "We've all agreed to dispense with titles amongst ourselves. If you've no objection?"

"Not in the slightest."

"Fine." She adjusted her feet. "You're most welcome to join our estate tour at any point, Emryn. I look forward to it." She glanced at her group. "If you're ready, we'll be going." Spreading her wings, she lifted off and led her fluttering charges down the drive. "First stop: the gatehouse to get you all registered and acquainted with procedure for leaving the estate, should you wish."

Kerrigold fell into flight beside her. "Forgive my bluntness, Lyssica, but does it feel strange being the heir?"

"Yes and no." Lyssica gestured with one hand. "The heir's always been my brother, DeMaksim, so that's the 'yes' part."

"And the 'no' part?" Kerrigold side-swooped a tree to snag an autumn leaf.

"Estate management is something I find interesting. I love nurturing animals and plants, and I see this as similar, so stepping into the heir's shoes was excellent for me."

Kerrigold nodded. "So you're happy in the role." She pleated the leaf between slim fingers. "I'm a craft artist, so managing an estate wouldn't suit me at all. I don't have the least interest in it, but my family believes learning new skills will broaden my appeal as a consort match. We made a deal that I give the program a go in exchange for some personal bonuses."

"You should talk with Zhu more – she's the artist in our family."

"Yes." Kerrigold's eyes sparkled. "I admire her work immensely and I'd love to make my art into a business. I agreed to this placement above all those I was offered because of your sister's proximity. With three moons of time here, I'm hoping to meet her informally and obtain professional artistic advice."

"I'm certain that can be organised." Lyssica landed outside the gate house and reached for the door, but a male hand beat her to it.

"Allow me, Lyssica." Venaday Tortrician smirked at her as he folded his wings. Lyssica restrained her urge to kick him with great difficulty. She'd been hurt the evening before and he'd seen it as a chance to recite trite poetry? He hadn't changed at all. Digging her fingernails into her palms, she kept her voice cool.

"My thanks, Venaday. Very nice of you to hold the door open for everyone." His smirk sagged as she swept past, as regally as one could while limping, and was followed by Kerrigold.

"But..."

"Thanks Ven." Melkaz Eriocraan breezed by, closely shadowed by Tanjil and Perris, leaving a scowling Venaday to bring up the rear. Forcing herself to keep a straight face, Lyssica shepherded her party to the reception desk.

"Greetings Lozito, how are you?"

"Very well, thanks, Lady Lyssica." The snub-nosed guard tucked a loose lock of flaxen hair behind a pointy ear then flipped open the day book. "I take it these are our Tri-moon guests?"

"Yes." Lyssica rearranged a vase of wilting flowers, righting a petal here and stretching to smooth a calyx on the other side. "Could you record their information please? Make a note they have live-in guest rights for the duration of their stay." Turning to her charges, she waved to encompass the office.

"This is where you come if you're wanting to leave the estate. You sign out and then sign in upon your return." She smiled. "It sounds straight forward, but search parties don't wish to have their time wasted. This kind of detail is important in the running of a large estate, as some of you may already know, so don't forget." One by one, they came up, provided their data and moved outside to wait. Lyssica was last out. Satisfaction filled her as her final glance at the vase of flowers showed them looking fresh and perky.

As she passed, Perris caught her arm. "We need to speak privately, Lyssica."

Fighting not to shudder, she pulled her arm free. "I'm certain we'll have the chance at some point." Smiling tightly, she turned away. "But for now, we'll cut through these woods to the summer house. It used to be Zhu's studio before she moved to Garadenya Estate with her true-mate." She took to the air, her group following one at a time.

As they flitted along a path between large pine trees, Lyssica was glad to see Perris had fallen back to play a game of tag with Tanjil using a pine cone flinging it at each other around trees and branches. Although conducting a low-voiced conversation, Melkaz and Venaday kept an eye on the wildly played game, ducking or dodging several times, to avoid being hit.

Drawing up outside the outlying building, Lyssica gestured. "The summer house was designed by famous Fae-architect, Sir Feragamo Notodonkae." She hovered at the bottom of the stairs. "Note the sliding door and large glass window in the 'valiant' style. Anyone wish to look inside? No? Okay then, let's keep going." She struck off through the small forest, a band of which bordered the estate on three sides. "This way to the formal gardens. The first one we'll come to is—"

"Aargh!" Lord Tanjil Blastobarm's yell came from behind a large pine tree. "Aargh! Aargh! By the Goddess, aargh!" With each screech his voice got louder and louder. Kerrigold froze, while Lyssica, Melkaz and Venaday all zoomed around the tree to discover the cause of his yelling.

Kneeling in a mass of muddy pine needles, Tanjil pointed at the base of a large tree trunk, eyes round with horror. A pale-faced Perris hovered nearby, pine cone in one hand, his mouth hanging open. From the narrow opening in the hollow cavity of an ancient tree, a white hand protruded, palm up, fingers pointing skyward. The ground was torn up and pockmarked with drag marks leading towards the trunk's gaping maw.

"Enough, Tanjil!" Lyssica shook his shoulder, but his mouth was a rictus of fear from which another wild bellow issued. Melkaz stepped closer and slapped Tanjil across the face. His eyes bulged even more, before he crumpled, a harsh sob escaping him. Lyssica's mouth twisted; the Fae were a long-lived race so death was often simply a word rather than a reality.

Perris lowered the pine cone, hand shaking, face pale as he stared at Lyssica. "Who is it?"

She sighed. "I've never made a study of hands, Perris. I'll have to look."

"It's got to be someone from your estate." He swallowed. "And you're the only one here familiar with all of your people."

Perhaps so, but really! From a hand? She flew across the messy ground and approached the trunk's narrow hollow, twisting to hover alongside. The body was stuffed into the cavity at an awkward angle. One arm thrust out from the torso, resulting in the hand extending through the opening. Lyssica recognised what she could see of the clothing as the outfit worn by Roland Arrelgyre the previous night, but he was lying face down. Further, the head was covered by a hood, making it impossible for a clear identification and, hadn't Roland left early this morning?

"Well?" Venaday's voice was sharp with demand. "Is there someone attached to the hand?"

Kerrigold's face appeared from beyond her concealing tree trunk. "Really Venaday! Do you think there are random hands lying around in the woods?"

"Well, there could be!" His hands went to his hips. "Art is done here, there might be hand statuary at random places."

Perris sighed. "I think Lyssica would've said something were that the case."

"You think?" Venaday pursed his lips and emitted a rasping blurt. "That's ridiculous and so are you."

"You mannerless oaf!"

"Get over it." Venaday shrugged. "Well Lyssica? Is there a body joined to the hand?"

"Yes." Lyssica shuddered, because there definitely *was* a body and Venaday Tortrician was a disrespectful, blithering idiot who'd grated on her every nerve from the instant they'd met several years ago. *Thank the Goddess Ostara, I only have to endure the fool for three moons.*

She bit her lip; she would've followed emergency procedures, but, since the unfortunate squashed into the hollow of the tree hadn't responded to the loud disagreement, she didn't think there was any point. "Kerrigold, would you return to the manor and get Papan, please?"

"Of course." Kerrigold flitted upwards, then put on a burst of speed and shot away between the trees.

Melkaz fluttered closer. "Should we try and pull the body out of that hollow?" His expression was uneasy, flicking from her to Venaday to Tanjil to Perris and back again.

"No. We touch nothing before Papan arrives."

Perris crouched down to check on Tanjil, who was now rocking himself to-and-fro.

"I know!" Venaday tapped his chest. "I'll start a business as a private investigator and this can be my first case." He grinned and swept a bow. "PI Venaday Tortrician at your service. Stand aside, Lyssica, let me study the body."

"No. Back off." Lyssica pinched the bridge of her nose. Was everything a performance, or a game, to this lackwit?

"But—"

She pinned him with a withering stare. "We'll await Papan." Turning away, she laid a hand on the tree trunk and almost hissed at the wrongness radiating from its heart. It was aware of something ugly befouling its space and wanted the thing removed. Like an infected splinter. She puzzled over a dead body classed as an ugly infection – was this connected to the infection problem she'd noticed in the garden and the forest? She had not arrived at an answer when the flutter of multiple wing-beats broke what had become an uneasy silence.

An instant later, her father, Dario, Kerrigold and two guards cleared the tops of the trees. They landed, one after the other, pausing to fold their wings before approaching. Bursting from the woods in a steady, ground eating lope came a large, maned wildcat with a pair of wicked looking horns. When none of the males paid attention, Lyssica deduced the huge brown and tan animal to be Emryn. She was disappointed when he stopped behind a large tree and reappeared a few moments later, a fully dressed Fae-male. He had a pack slung over one shoulder. A clothing bag? Either he'd carried it or someone had dropped it there for him to find; too bad it robbed her of what she was certain would be a very fine view of his naked muscled body.

Her father stopped beside her. "What's going on? Kerrigold said there's a body?"

"Yes, father."

Duke Yanvian absorbed Lyssica's report before moving to the tree for a closer look. "We'll have to bring the body out." He nodded at the two guards. "Vynstan, Brom would you assist me?"

Dario moved forward. "Let Emryn and I help in place of you, Yanvian. No offence meant, but we have the suppleness of youth on our side and four will make it even easier."

"Good points. I'm not offended." The duke stayed with Lyssica as the four Fae-males moved to liberate the body. Vynstan grasped the protruding hand, while Brom eased an arm into the hollow around the shoulders. The pair twisted and wriggled the torso until it came free, then Emryn came in on one side and Dario the other, to help free the hips and legs.

Laid flat on the ground, the limp figure drew everyone like iron filings to a magnet. Somebody whimpered; it could have been Tanjil.

Lyssica swallowed. "There's something strange here." Her goddess senses were shrieking and it wasn't simply because the head was completely encased in a hood.

Perris tugged an earlobe. "Well, those are the clothes Roland Arrelgyre was wearing last night, but what's with the hood?" The head covering was secured by wide ribbons tied in a bow under the chin.

"And the ribbon bow ..." Kerrigold's voice faded as Vynstan bent, untying the ribbons. The hood loosened and Brom put a hand under the head then drew the fabric free. They all stared down at the greyed, sunken face, wide staring eyes, the mouth ajar in a silent scream.

"It's definitely Roland." Melkaz sounded shaken. "But how'd he die?"

Tanjil's voice trembled. "I can't see any b-blood."

Leaning forward, Dario opened the shirt collar and eased the material aside to check the neck. "No bruising."

Kerrigold pointed at the hood. "Maybe that was used to suffocate him?" Before anyone could answer, a shaft of sunlight broke through the trees, illuminating the dimness and silhouetting Emryn against the bright glow.

Duke Yanvian gestured. "Could you move a little, Emryn? Give us better light?"

"Sure." He stepped aside, allowing the sunbeam to fully illuminate Roland's body; lifeless, waxy grey skin and distorted features on a body completely clothed, except for boots.

"What—"

The corpse brightened suddenly, sparks rising above it, flashing like fireflies. The guards near the body edged back, as did Dario. The grey face began to glow as if lit from within. The skin cracked, peeled and tore, allowing gleams of light to shoot through the gaps. The face sloughed off like serpent skin, the eyes popped out and one after another, the teeth shot out of the mouth as if propelled. Blond hair blackened and the darkness spread, over the forehead, down the blazing face and under the chin to disappear into the open neck of the shirt.

The creature sat up. The spears of light highlighted the flesh of the face, reforming it like moulded wax until it no longer resembled Roland Arrelgyre. White clawed paws pushed eyes back into sockets above a prominent, be-whiskered snout. The eyes swivelled to focus on the stunned and horrified watchers, assessing each one in turn. When it's malignant gaze landed on Lyssica, the hare-like creature grinned, revealing new sharp teeth, front and centre in the top jaw. It shook its head, tossing long, floppy ears to-and-fro, then scrabbled to stand upright. Filled with apprehension, Lyssica drew a cloak of Ostara's fertile life force around herself.

"Greetings, Chosen of Ostara, from the Bodach." The hare bowed, then straightened. Its head tilted, a white paw stroked long black whiskers as it regarded Lyssica almost slyly. "He hopes you enjoyed the show." The other paw tossed a cloud of glittering dust towards her, but Emryn leapt, grasped her arm and jerked her out of reach.

A fireball formed in the hand of Dario, the Unseelie Beast, and he flung it at the black and white furred thing. The rabbity creature gave Lyssica a wave and a smirking, toothy grin before the explosion knocked everyone flat.

When the dust cleared and they raised themselves to look, there was no trace – the rabbit-hare had vanished.

CHAPTER SIX

EMRYN

*E*mryn couldn't stop running his hands over Lyssica. Kynthcat, a surge of fur and claw within him, was also demanding to see and feel her. "Lyssica! Are you hurt?"

Her hands rose to bat at his, a shaky smile briefly curling her lips. "Thank you, I'm fine. You don't need to ..." She stopped, swallowing whatever she'd been about to say, then her voice emerged as a whisper. "That awful creature with its strange dust."

He shook his head. Voices floated to them on the ether.

"What just happened?"

"What in the name of the Goddess, was that?"

Dario snarled; a new fireball flaming on his fingertips. "By Old Mab's teeth and hair! It's gone!"

Kerrigold wrung her hands. "Your fire probably killed it!"

"Singed it maybe." Dario shook his head. "No, it got away."

Teeth clenched, Emryn joined everyone else in staring at the slightly scorched, bare ground. There was no body, no body parts, no discarded clothing, only blackened earth where the leaf litter and sparse blades of grass had exploded into a conflagration.

Engaging the heightened, but enraged senses of Kynthcat, Emryn moved closer, sniffing and pushing his tongue out to taste the air. A stench of black snow and putrid mud assailed him, over-powering the burnt smell. His tongue curled in disgust. He spat, then blinked his alternate vision into play – and there were the sparkling remnants of the glitter dust the creature had hurled at Lyssica. It was eating into the charred ground making the area worse by the second. Emryn could think of only one way to stop the blight.

"Dario!" He pointed. "Firebomb that black spot – the glitter dust that thing threw is disintegrating everything it touches."

Dario nodded. "Everyone, stand back." Body tense, he hurled another fireball.

Alternate vision still focusing, Emryn watched the firebomb land. A dark section in the middle of the blighted ground burst into flame. It roared high in a gout of black flame, lowered to a sullen grey, then changed to the colours of true fire before it finally snuffed out. Staring intently, Emryn realised the problem wasn't over yet. "Keep going Dario! Start where the edges meet the healthy ground and ring the entire portion of affected earth. What you did worked, but the blight is spreading outwards. We must stop it before the entire forest is ruined."

Mouth a thin line, Dario enflamed his second hand and took turns aiming fireballs in the pattern Emryn advised. Smoke wreathed the surrounds and coughing broke out amongst the watching Fae-folk.

Emryn's heavy exhaled breath was redolent with frustration; the stink of fear from the estate visitors combined with their macabre fascination, masked any other scents he might pick up. He glanced around, alert in case the thing returned.

Tanjil's back was plastered against a tree trunk; tears trickled down his cheeks as he rocked himself. Kerrigold talked to him quietly, gently clasping his arm.

Melkaz and Perris alternated glances between Dario, Emryn and the blighted ground. Venaday, mouth open, didn't stop staring at the fiery Dario. Duke Yanvian strode out from where he'd been searching among nearby trees. Meeting Emryn's gaze, he shook his head.

"No signs of the thing anywhere in the vicinity." Eyes widening, the Duke of Papillion stepped back as his son-in-law aimed and cast another fireball.

Hands still aflame, Dario strode closer to the blackened ground. "Emryn? Do I need to continue?" Emryn assessed the ground, looking for any further glitterdust. Lyssica answered before he could.

"It's all gone." Hands spread in front of her, eyes closed, she faced the blight. Her actions garnered everyone's attention.

Dario cast her an interested look; Yanvian awarded a dubious frown. They both raised eyebrows at Emryn, who nodded. "She's right."

Duke Yanvian confronted his eldest daughter. "Just exactly how do *you* know that, Lyssica? With your eyes shut?"

Lyssica nibbled on her bottom lip, then squinted at him, her gaze troubled.

The duke pinched the bridge of his nose. "Not to mention, I was summoned here because of a body in a hollow tree, believed to be Roland Arrelgyre. I thought that highly unlikely since I saw him out through the front gate and on his way home early this morning, yet here he was." He gestured violently at the scorched earth. "Him, or something that started off looking like him, until it became what? Some type of malevolent, bi-coloured, oversized rabbit thing?"

Lyssica stared at the blight, brows knit.

Dario peered at her. "Whatever it was, it seemed to recognise you, Lyss, and not in a good way. Judging by how the dust affected the ground, Emryn just saved your life."

Lyssica's troubled gaze lifted to tangle with Emryn's. "That's true." She didn't look away. "Thank you for that."

"More than a pleasure." Her eyes beckoned. Opening his senses wide, he reached for the link, wrapping himself in it. Their gazes held.

Kynthcat preened. *'She like us. Me like her, you do too.'*

Ignoring his outrageous cat, he cleared his throat and found his voice, enthralled by those captivating doe eyes. "It targeted you, that's for certain. If that's the case it'll be back."

Kerrigold swung around. "Why didn't you stop it?" Her sudden movement startled Emryn out of his private moment with Lyssica.

"We tried." Duke Yanvian shook his head. "It vanished using dark magic. The rest was smoke and mirrors with a finishing touch of poisonous dust."

Dario extinguished the flame of his Unseelie Beast, shook his hands out and straightened the cuffs of his jacket. "I agree."

Melkaz cleared his throat. "Perhaps it wanted us to think it had died?"

"Ooh!" Venaday rubbed his palms together. "What a great thought, Melkaz – I'll include that in my notes later."

Duke Yanvian raised a supercilious eyebrow. "Notes?"

Venaday performed a flowery bow. "Venaday Tortrician, Private Investigator – my new career, you know." The Fae-male touched a finger to the side of his nose and winked. "Nothing to fear now that I'm on the case."

Grimacing as he looked away, Emryn discovered Dario smirking at him. His new mentor raised one hand to the side of his head and circled a finger several times, his gaze flicking to Venaday and back. Emryn hid his answering grin behind one hand.

Yanvian snorted. "Private investigations into this thing will get you killed, Venaday Tortrician. If you want to go home alive after this Tri-moon program, you'll refrain from doing anything so foolhardy. I have no wish to send home pieces of you in a coffin."

Dario studied the ground, head tilted. "I can't help wondering – was this really Roland Arrelgyre? Or simply a magical impersonation?"

Perris pressed fingers to his forehead, massaging. "If that's the case, it was an excellent impersonation of Roland."

Kerrigold nodded. "Therefore it had to have at least seen him, but was it the kind of creature to leave him traveling on undisturbed?"

Emryn snorted. "No. It was full of innate cunning, with a highlight of viciousness." His shudder was instinctive.

Melkaz studied him. "How do you know that?"

Emryn cast him a sidelong glance; he'd have to reveal a part of his nature to answer that question. "Empath."

An expression of outrage moulded Venaday's face. "So you constantly sense our feelings? Is there no privacy?"

"That's incorrect." Emryn frowned. Why did everyone always leap to that conclusion? "Generally, everybody has a personal mind shield through which I don't intrude unless invited, but violent or sudden feelings and thoughts are broadcast so loudly that they trample personal shields and in such situations I can't avoid hearing things." He nodded towards the scorch mark. "In the case of *that* creature, it didn't care who could hear it."

Duke Yanvian, hands at chest height, tapped fingertips together. "I'll need to send out search parties to look for Arrelgyre, or his belongings. We must ascertain whether the body here was really him, or a magical cover the creature superimposed over its true shape."

Lyssica wrinkled her nose. "You are assuming the nasty rabbit persona is its true shape."

Duke Yanvian's eyes narrowed. "And you don't?"

She tilted her head. "Well, maybe, but maybe not."

"Not very clear."

"It's more what the thing represents. Real rabbits don't behave like that. Ergo, it was a magical construct of some sort, sent by someone else."

Her father pursed his lips, still glaring. "Any idea who?"

Lyssica spread her hands. "It did mention the Bodach, but who knows if that is true or not. What is clear is, it *was* targeting me."

"Yes." Dario stroked his chin. "It recognised you, didn't it? Why might that be?"

Wincing, Lyssica studied the blackened ground.

"Lyssica?" Emryn placed a gentle hand on her arm. She rewarded him with a tiny smile. "There are lives at stake, so if you know anything that could help us, we would appreciate you sharing the information."

She sighed. "It's because of what I do." She glanced around the group.

Emryn did also, noting the prevalence of scowling faces. "You know, if frowns were people, there'd be a nasty crowd here right now."

Duke Yanvian folded his arms. "Keep going, Lyssica. That requires explaining."

She faced him; her mouth opened and closed, then she glanced around as if waiting for something. Finally she shrugged. "I'm a Handmaiden of Ostara. I have been since I was seven."

The Duke of Papillion looked like somebody had hit him over the head with a tree branch. "What! Why is this the first I've heard of it?"

Lyssica's throat worked; her voice emerged shaky and low. "Ostara bespelled me to silence for my own protection. The fact that I am now able to reveal the truth reinforces my belief that something is seriously wrong."

"That's right." Dario's hands went to his hips. "The rabbit thing called you 'Chosen of Ostara'. That's why you were the focus."

Emryn 's brow furrowed. "But it makes no sense. Rabbits are a symbol of Ostara and her fertility aspect, so why was the creature in rabbit form? A murderous rabbit? That's an antithesis."

Lyssica rubbed her temples. "Unless you're mocking the Goddess."

Duke Yanvian threw his hands in the air. "But you're Seelie and Ostara is an Unseelie Goddess!"

Emryn winced, but Lyssica pinned her father with a glare. "You forget yourself, Papan! Seelie and Unseelie are a United race under the joint Queendom and, if you recall, you fought in the Fae Wars for Fae Unity. You have both a son-in-law and a daughter-in-law who are both Unseelie. Your reaction is the very reason my silence on the matter was enforced by Ostara."

"Damn, you're right." Her father sighed as he focused on Dario, then glanced at Emryn. "My apologies. Old habits are harder to break than I realised."

Dario waved a hand. "Luckily I know you better than you think I do, old goat. I'm ignoring it."

Emryn nodded. "I'm taking Dario's answer for my own. If he says it's okay, then it is."

"Thank you." Yanvian swallowed as he turned to Lyssica again. "So, you're working for an Uns ... Ah, that is, you're working for a goddess and because of it, a monster is making you the object of its malevolence?"

Lyssica bared her teeth in a fierce smile. "That about sums it up, Papan." Emryn wanted to applaud. He hid his grin, but shite, she was a fierce little thing. She looked all fluffy and adorable like a kitten wanting to be stroked and cuddled, until her hidden claws came out to slash the unwary.

'Mmroww!' Kynthcat's tail flicked him. 'Fierce kitten ours.'

CHAPTER SEVEN

LYSSICA

Flitting back to the manor house, Lyssica's thoughts were whirling. *'Papan will want more information. How much should I explain? How much do I want to explain? How can I explain?* Her stomach twisted uneasily. Her role as Ostara's Handmaiden was a secret she'd been forced to conceal for years for her own protection. But the spell, which had stopped admissions on her part, whether inadvertent or purposeful, was gone. Now what?

Next to her, Papan bellowed orders even as he aimed for his personal study. "I want a squad of guards to search the Great West Road for Roland Arrelgyre! Brom, you're in charge of them. Vynstan, you take another squad and comb the estate for that rabbit-hare thing, or anything you think suspicious."

Lyssica combed fingers through her hair. Images of the horrible rabbit poking its eyes back in filled her mind; the creature's disrespectful use of Ostara's symbol sickened her, but it was also a warning. *I need to go to the Forest Circle as soon as I can, make my territory defences stronger. Even though I've already begun the winter protection rites, I must contact Ostara for further assistance and advice. This matter is so far beyond my expertise it's not funny.*

"Erm, Lyssica?"

Recognising Dario's voice, she glanced up. He surreptitiously indicated the five program apprentices milling uncertainly in the foyer, casting either anxious or speculative glances at her. She was pleased to have him and Emryn standing like sentinels on either side of her; two big, brawny males helping her feel safe, while Entanglit held his position at the entry. However, as the only family member here, it was time to play host.

Lyssica clapped her hands. "Right. Let's all go into the morning room and Entanglit will bring tea and biscuits. We can wind down and decide what's next on the agenda." She looked to their majordomo. "If you wouldn't mind, Entanglit?"

He bowed. "Certainly Lady Lyssica. Tea and biscuits in a jiffy." He strode off down the hallway.

The group adjourned to the morning room in silence and took seats where they could see her. Relief filled Lyssica as Emryn came to stand beside the chair she'd chosen while Dario took a position near the door. She scanned the uneasy faces, coming to Melkaz last. He pinned her with a stare. "Will the program continue now that one of us has been murdered?"

Lyssica dug fingernails into her palms. "I won't make any decisions without Papan's input. I'd like it to continue, but it may come back to personal preferences. For now, we're safe and every effort will be made to ensure that continues."

"But Roland—"

"Made his own path with his unrelenting bigotry." Emryn cut in. "That he came to grief afterwards is not something anyone expected or could have predicted." The electric silence that ensued was broken by a light tap at the door.

"Argh!" Tanjil Blastobarm started violently, then continued to shake like a leaf in wind. When the door opened for Entanglit to propel his tea trolley into the room, Tanjil sagged, his Adam's apple moving in an agitated swallow.

Lyssica hastily poured a cup of tea, added plenty of sugar and passed it over. "Here Tanjil, the tea will do you good. Would you like a biscuit too?" Entanglit proffered the biscuit tray to Tanjil, but he shook his head, clutching his tea cup like a lifeline.

"N-no thanks."

Lyssica continued to pour tea until everyone was served. Even with tea in hand, Emryn remained steadfast at her elbow; she cast him a grateful smile, unable to stop admiring him despite the circumstances. He was such a tower of strength and she'd been attracted from the beginning. She pulled a face – she'd fallen into his arms. Could a meeting be any more cliché than that? Turning, she watched Entanglit move from person to person with the biscuit tray, until the room was quiet except for the sipping of tea and the munching of cookies.

When the door opened to admit Papan, Tanjil trembled so much he dropped his cup.

"It's just the duke, Tanjil." Kerrigold patted his arm. Entanglit recovered the cup and mopped the few spilled drops.

Lyssica placed her cup on the trolley. "Tea, Papan?"

"Yes, thank you, Lyssica." He waited as she poured a cup, then paced to the nearby fireplace and set it on the mantelpiece. "I assume everyone has questions, so let's talk. I have sent guards to look for signs of Roland Arrelgyre in case the creature was impersonating him."

Melkaz cleared his throat. "I've already asked Lyssica, but she said to wait for your input, so I ask again: Will the program be continuing after this apparent murder of one of us?"

The duke clasped his hands behind his back. "I'll not stop anyone who wishes to leave and I'll provide an armed escort. Having said that, I'd like the program to continue – I'll remind you we all signed contracts—"

Perris frowned. "We did, but we had no idea a murder would happen."

Duke Yanvian inclined his head. "Correct. There is a clause in the contract to cover unexpected circumstances, so as I've just said, whoever wants to leave may do so."

"I can't stay here!" Tanjil's lips twisted. "I want to go home."

"Very well." Duke Yanvian looked from Kerrigold, to Perris, Melkaz, then Venaday. "Anyone else?"

"Oh, I'm definitely staying." Venaday leaned forward. "My PI investigation needs me to be front and centre."

When Emryn gently nudged her, Lyssica pressed her lips together, staring into her cup. Don't laugh. Once she had herself firmly under control, she looked up, only to meet Dario's grinning gaze; he pointed a finger at the side of his head and moved it in a circle. She choked and squeezed her eyes shut. Damn the pair of them!

Kerrigold's voice filled the room. "I'd like time to think about it."

Lyssica drew breath. "What if everyone takes the rest of the day to consider, then announces their choice over breakfast tomorrow?" Murmurs of agreement came.

The duke nodded. "An excellent idea. We'll leave it there, shall we?"

Perris looked between Lyssica and her father. "And you'll keep us apprised of anything you discover about Roland?"

"Don't doubt it." Duke Yanvian focused on Lyssica. "Now, we need to go to my office so you can you explain more about being a 'Handmaiden of Ostara', Lyssica."

She faced him. "I'm happy to talk about it, but we'll stay here." She'd prefer a public discussion. "I've nothing to hide, in fact I'm proud of my role, so what is it you wish to know?"

"How did she contact you?"

"I was seven, singing and dancing in the forest. Maman had taken all of us to the stone circle the previous day and I'd loved it so much I went back by myself. Ostara appeared as a tiny-winged Fae, joined in with me, then complimented me on my skills and introduced herself as Ostara, The Spring Fairy. She talked about how much work she had to do and I offered to help. She accepted my offer and I've been her Handmaiden ever since."

The duke rubbed his chin. "What does being a Handmaiden entail?"

"Looking after the flora and fauna in this region." Lyssica tilted her head. "I suppose you could say I'm her area representative."

Her father's frown deepened. "How do you do whatever it is you do? And where?"

Lyssica returned his frown. "There are some things that are between Ostara and me. As to where, I go to the forest outside our estate most afternoons to help any plants or animals in need. Ostara is the Goddess of Spring, Dawn and Fertility, with the hare as her symbol – but we've covered that already."

Papan gritted his teeth. "With that rabbit monster around, it's not safe. You will cease your visits to the forest."

Lyssica clenched her fists. "I will *not*. I swore an oath and I have responsibilities to fulfill. If you give me a moment I'll contact the Goddess Ostara for advice."

Her father's eyebrows raised. "We don't have time for you to set up some elaborate folderol ceremony with candles and scent sticks, then go into a trance, or whatever it is you do. The situation is critical and—"

"That's rubbish." Closing her eyes, Lyssica tuned her father out, took five deep breaths, envisaged their virtual meeting room in her mind and went inside. She created an image of Ostara's face, sent her mind call down their pathway, just as she always did, and waited.

And waited.

And waited some more.

'How strange. Ostara usually responds promptly.' She sent another call down their link, focusing more deeply in hope of an answer. The increased depth of her awareness revealed an unusual thick fog swallowing her calls, murky tendrils now reaching towards her. Uneasily, she backed out of the virtual meeting room and opened her eyes.

Everyone watched her, fascination written across their faces. Lyssica firmed her mouth and met her father's green and violet gaze.

"Well?"

She shook her head. "I couldn't reach her. I'm being blocked."

"What do you mean, 'blocked'?"

She drummed her fingers on the tea tray. "There was a fog and it was … in between me and where I wanted to go." Her frown deepened. "But it was also like I was being surrounded. Trapped even. It wasn't a pleasant sensation. I'll try again later."

"Is that wise?" Emryn asked.

Her gaze met his worried one. Instead of annoying her, his worry was like a balm. Even so, she spoke firmly. "I made a vow I have no wish to break."

Emryn nodded. "I admire your dedication." His words tingled pleasantly through her and she rewarded him with a smile.

Dario sauntered over and poured himself more tea. "There is something of deceit and trickery about all of this. What do you know about the Bodach?"

Lyssica's nose wrinkled. "The Bodach? He's the consort of the Cailleach."

Kerrigold leaned forward. "The Cailleach? You mean the Goddess of Winter?"

"Technically, she's Goddess of the Winds and the Cold, often called the Queen of Winter, or the Veiled One." Lyssica twisted her fingers in her skirts. "Her consort, the Bodach, is not a god, but he is a prankster. Unfortunately what he thinks amusing, others can find unpleasant, even deadly."

"And the Cailleach doesn't stop him?"

Lyssica shook her head. "She doesn't always know what he's doing. He's sly and secretive, and she's a fair and just deity, dedicated to doing right. I'm not sure how they came to be paired."

Melkaz lowered his teacup to his saucer. "If you're a Handmaiden of Ostara, how do you know so much about winter's deities?"

Lyssica shrugged. "Spring follows winter. Ostara takes over from the Cailleach and they talk. Sometimes they engage in contests which result in overlapping seasons. Ostara ushers in more clement weather and a thaw starts. The Cailleach responds by flinging more snow. Ostara organises warm winds and Spring rains. The Cailleach's answer is to force the temperature down and change the rain to sleet and ice. That sort of thing. You've all experienced such weather." She glanced around; they were all staring.

Suddenly Venaday rubbed his hands together. "This is wonderful! You're beautiful and you know two goddesses – it's perfect!"

Lyssica stared, fighting disbelief. What was the idiot warbling about? "Thank you for the compliment, but what's your point?"

He beamed. "I hadn't thought you'd be a good enough match for me. My family is quite exalted, you know. Pure bloodlines. We vet a prospect carefully before inviting them to join us. But you! Working with one goddess and knowing a second one – that elevates your importance well above the demarcation line. You qualify easily." He leapt from his seat, approached with firm strides and grasped a hand. "I offer myself to you. We won't want to waste any time, so I'm sure a consorting ceremony can be arranged easily and quickly." He patted her hand, started massaging her fingers.

A low growl came from behind her. Lyssica ignored it and withdrew her hand from his pawing clasp. He reached for it again, but she held it up between them, palm facing him. "No."

"No?" His mouth dropped open. He closed it with a snap. "What do you mean?"

"It's very kind of you to offer, but I have no desire to be your consort or have you as mine, so, no. Thank you."

He stared at her, brows so high they were covered by his hair. Then he relaxed, uttering a brief laugh. "I get it. You're shy. I've embarrassed you in front of all these onlookers. No matter. I'll approach the subject with you later, in private."

Lyssica sighed. "Lord Venaday, you force me to be blunt. I'm not currently seeking a consort, but even if I were, you're not whom I would choose. I'm sorry to disappoint you, but you don't have the qualities I want."

Before anything else could be said, Emryn moved purposefully forward, snarling. "This is irrelevant." The glare he aimed at Venaday promised blood. "Lyssica is in danger and must be protected and yet you mock her." His glowing eyes bounced from Duke Yanvian to Dario. "The Bodach named her – he has her in his sights and he's dangerous." His top lip wrinkled, then his smouldering gaze fastened on Lyssica and she fought a tremble of pleasure. It was like being exposed to a furnace – and it felt sooo good.

"Exactly!" Dario moved to flank Emryn. "She needs a guard."

"Excellent idea!" Duke Yanvian nodded firmly.

Lyssica wanted to protest, but she knew they were right. *The Bodach is up to something and I won't be able to protect myself properly while I'm engrossed in my duties. Papan already said he doesn't want me going to the forest – wait a minute.* She lowered her hand to cover the smile fighting to break free and cleared her throat.

Her father glowered. "No. Arguments."

"Have I argued?" She clasped a hand to the base of her throat. "I will happily accept and cooperate with a guard – if you stop trying to prevent me going to the forest to carry out my handmaiden duties." His eyes narrowed as he studied her. She stared resolutely back at him.

Finally he nodded. "Deal."

She smiled. "Thank you Papan." *I won't tell him I'd have done what I want regardless of his commands.*

Emryn took a step forward. "I will—"

Perris stepped in front of him. "I'd be happy to guard Lyssica."

"No!" Lyssica swallowed bile. She'd flee before ever again entrusting her safety to Perris.

His smile faltered. "What do you mean, no? There's nobody else here who could look after you like I can."

She shook her head, edging away from him when he reached for her. "No!"

Emryn stepped between them, body tense. "Are you always so rude Perris?" A low growl emanated from his chest.

Perris's Adam's apple bobbed. "Rude? It's not rude to state a truth. Lyssica needs—"

"You don't know what I need." Fingers clenching, her gaze

flickered to Emryn then back to Perris. "I mean ... I ... we couldn't ask that of you," she finally managed to blurt out.

Papan studied her – she endeavoured not to tremble in the face of his assessing gaze. But after a moment he simply turned to Perris and said, "Thank you Perris, but I think Emryn would be our best choice. He's a warrior where you're not. I won't have someone with less than basic training protecting my daughter."

Perris shook his head. "I've had basic training!"

"It's not enough." Papan nodded as he turned to Emryn. "I'd like you to be Lyssica's guard, Emryn. Is that acceptable to you?"

Emryn pressed his chest with a clenched fist. "It would be my honour, Your Grace." Perris swung on his heel and stalked from the room; the door slammed behind him.

Lyssica heaved a sigh. *Thank the Goddess.* Hoping nobody noticed her hands trembling, she endeavoured to focus as her father continued.

"Dario, what say you?"

"It's a great idea; we'll need to work around Emryn's contractual expectations, though."

Papan steepled his fingers and tapped his thumbs together. "Fine. Let's hammer out the details."

Dario stroked his chin. "Okay, we know Emryn must spend time mentoring with me and Lyssica is involved with instructing the Papillion apprentices, so needs to be here. Then, there's her goddess-given tasks in the forest, a part of which stretches between our estates." Dario glanced from Yanvian to Lyssica and on to Emryn. "So, if the guarding is to be successful, Emryn must stay with Lyssica full time."

Lyssica's eyes widened. "What? Why? Surely, he could just come here early in the day while I do my work, then accompany me to the forest and back before he returns to Garadenya Island in the afternoon to complete his tasks?" Although whichever way things went, she'd get to spend a lot more time in Emryn's company and that pleased her no end. She fought to keep her smile hidden.

Papan frowned. "Will that work?"

Brows knit, Dario glanced between them. "I doubt it. I'm sorry Lyssica, but what you suggest wastes a lot of time. Besides, you can't possibly stay alone in your tower– it's too easy to access from the outside."

"Well, Papan could put guards—"

"And take them away from their other duties?" Emryn pursed his lips. "Or are you proposing they do longer hours, further exhausting them when your Papan needs them all more focused, rather than less?"

"I—"

Dario shook his head. "Emryn is right, Lyss,"

Papan crossed his arms. "Then how is this going to work?"

Dario clasped his hands behind his back. "I propose Lyss comes to stay with us."

Lyssica's eyes widened. "What? I can't possibly—"

Dario held up his hand. "Hear me out. If you come to stay with us, Emryn and I can do our work early in the morning while Lyss and Zhu keep each other company. Then Emryn and Lyssica can return here late morning." Dario raised his eyes to his father-in-law. "That's the time she'll help with your Tri-moon guests. Mid-afternoon, they both leave here and return to Garadenya via the forest where Lyssica can complete whatever responsibilities necessary before they return to Garadenya for the night. We have a suite with a bedroom only accessible through a smaller antechamber." He turned to Lyssica. "We'll put you in the bedroom and have Emryn in the antechamber to keep you safe.'" He paused. "Thoughts?"

It really was quite sensible. And it would enable her to get away from … No. She wouldn't even think his name. But she would be able to keep her distance and feel safer at night. Plus she would get to spend more time with Zhu … and Emryn. Hoping nobody noticed the hot flush suffusing her body at that thought, she nodded primly. "That will work. Thank you Dario, I accept." She glanced across the room. "Emryn?"

Gleaming eyes meshed with hers. He inclined his head. "I also find these arrangements acceptable."

"Great!" Lyssica's smiled brightly. "When do we begin?"

The duke's voice was pure steel.

"Now."

CHAPTER EIGHT

EMRYN

*E*mryn braced against the cold winds blustering from a louring sky as he stood on the front verandah of the Papillion Estate manor house.. This last official day of autumn was bitter; he tasted oncoming snow within the chill gusts that whipped his cloak tighter around his legs. Although lunch was over and there were a few more hours before he and Lyssica usually set off to return to Garadenya Island, his senses warned him to leave early. Kynthcat agreed.

It was a good thing none of the other apprentices had decided to follow Tanjil's lead in scurrying home given the weather had turned colder and nastier the day after Roland Arrelgyre's unfortunate demise.

'He horrible male.'

'Yes – but nobody deserves to die that way.'

The guards had located his bags less than five leagues from the estate, ripped apart, the contents scattered. His wings had also been there, shredded and bloody, torn from his body by some unknown method. Arrelgyre had been flying home, but something had either dragged him from the sky or convinced him to land. Whether he'd been trapped or lured made little difference in the end. It had been a fatal choice, the cause of which continued to disturb them all.

Emryn had checked out the scene. The place was a mess of scent; Arrelgyre's was barely detectable over the revolting black snow and putrid mud smell of the devil-rabbit. There were other scents there, but Emryn was uneasy, because they were all a version of slimy wet fur, something with canine tendencies that he found unrecognisable. He pondered. Canine? Vulpine? He wasn't certain but the lingering presence of the stench indicated they were in league with the devil-rabbit and hence, the Bodach.

Anyone living on or near the estate had been warned of a killer on the loose. Descriptions of the magic using devil-rabbit had been circulated, with reports of any sightings requested and dispatches for the Queens, apprising them of the situation, had been sent along with a guard to the Arrelgyre family with a note from the duke and Roland's wings and belongings.

'Bad weather come soon,' Kynthcat reminded him. *'Need to take our lady and go.'*

Stalking back into the warmth of the Aphiski home, Emryn crossed to the work offices where Lyssica was seated at her desk with Kerrigold going over planning estimates and how she calculated them. He'd sat in on this lesson when she gave it to Perris, Venaday and Melkaz. Neither he nor Kynthcat liked the males near her, and there was no way he was leaving her alone with them like he did Kerrigold.

Melkaz wasn't so bad; he asked sensible questions and quickly grasped her teachings. Emryn was impressed at her knack of imparting information in an easily understood way. Perris had divided his attention between Lyssica and the watching Emryn, once even asking to see her privately. The question had been asked in a low voice, but Emryn, with his heightened shifter hearing, had no trouble picking it up. She had drawn Perris's notice back to the work and avoided answering.

Then, there was Venaday.

Emryn rolled his eyes. The obnoxious dolt made constant,

annoying interruptions, questioned Lyssica's methods and implied her strategies were flawed because she was female. He continued to importune Lyssica to consort with him on a daily basis – perhaps he was hoping to wear her resistance away. Kynthcat itched to gore the smarmy bastard. A low growl rumbled in his chest; the numpty severely tested his patience, never mind his self-restraint.

Emryn coughed to swallow his ire-inspired rumbling as Lyssica looked up enquiringly.

"Sorry for the interruption, but the weather is deteriorating. We need to leave now so you can still perform your Handmaiden magic in the forest before the oncoming storm."

"Oh, of course." Lyssica rose, closed the workbook and stacked some maps into a leather folder. "Kerrigold, we'll finish this tomorrow, if that suits?"

Her prompt response to his advice smothered the rest of Emryn's low burning annoyance. The constant proximity engendered by their recent roles as guard and target had earned her, not only his trust, but his respect – and she had just returned the compliment.

Kerrigold pushed back her chair. "Sure. The break will allow me to digest what you've already explained." She rubbed the back of her neck. "It's fascinating, but complicated. So much to consider. Thanks Lyssica. I'll see you tomorrow. You too, Emryn." She flashed a smile and left.

"I'd better inform Papan and grab my bag."

Emryn crossed to the inner door to Duke Yanvian's attached study. He knocked, opening the door almost simultaneously. The duke raised his head from paperwork, one brow lifting in enquiry.

"Lyssica and I are leaving now. There's a blizzard coming."

Yanvian stood immediately. "Thanks for the warning. I will tell my people to prepare. Make certain you and Lyssica stay safe. We may not have seen any new signs of the devil-rabbit or the Bodach in the last two weeks, but you can be sure they're still out there."

Emryn nodded. "Any new reports?"

Duke Yanvian snorted. "The creature's been seen in several different places at the same time. Either my Fae-folk are seeing things or there's a herd of the damned things on the loose."

Emryn shook his head. "Probably the first option. Folk are afraid."

"Yes." The duke dropped his pen and rubbed his eyes. "Go in safety."

"See you tomorrow, Papan." Lyssica called out as Emryn re-joined her.

"Ready?"

She nodded and led the way out of her office. In the foyer, they found Entanglit seated at his desk.

"I took the liberty of fetching your bag, Lady Lyssica. Miss Antigony had it packed and ready."

Lyssica smiled warmly. "Thank you, Entanglit. You're a gem. And would you please thank Tig for me?"

As she approached her pack on a table adjacent to the doors, Emryn ducked into an anteroom, stripped, stuffed his clothes in a waiting satchel and morphed into Kynthcat. The magic whisked through him, a flurry of light and nerve pulses that always left him alert and ready for anything.

'My turn.' Kynthcat gripped the satchel between his teeth, padded around the screen in place for his use and exited the anteroom.

Lyssica stood so that she could see both the anteroom door and Entanglit, to whom she was speaking. "Emryn sensed the bad weather approaching. A blizzard he said." She smiled as they appeared and relieved them of their satchel. "Papan is sending out warnings."

"I'll alert the household." Entanglit nodded. "And bar the doors after you leave. The weather already has an unpleasant aspect."

Indeed it did.

Lyssica must have felt it too as she stopped on top of the porch steps, tapping her pursed lips and studied the filthy sky. The wind buffeted her and ruffled Kynthcat's fur as he moved to place her on his lee side. He nudged her. She looked across, meeting his glowing silvery eyes. As Kynthcat, the top of his head was level with hers. He rumbled, waved a paw at the sky and shook his shaggy head.

She sighed. "You're right. The wind is already too strong for flying." Emryn had imposed the rule of low altitude flying very early in the arrangement, so Kynthcat could lope along beneath and still be close enough to protect her. In the two weeks since the guarding had begun, they'd worked out a steady, league covering pace which suited them both. Emryn had also planned strategies to follow should they be attacked, or some other emergency arise. He was pleased when she cooperated and put full effort into prac- tising the strategies with him. And his strange fascination with her continued to grow.

Rubbing a paw over one ear, he watched as she delved into her bag, pulled out her cloak and donned it. If she was flying, she preferred not to wear it, despite the wing-slits it contained. When she bent to pick up their bags, he uttered another low growl.

"Okay, okay." Leaning over him, she threaded a strap around his chest and buckled the bags in place. "I'll walk to the forest; it's not far." He grunted; he could deal with that.

Descending the steps, they set off down the driveway to the gatehouse. Even the postern gate was closed full time now, with a round-the-clock guard, the same as the main gates.

The curly headed Brom was on duty inside the building. "Leaving early today Lady Lyssica, Lord Emryn, Kynthcat?" Kynthcat rumbled a greeting.

"Snow storm on the way." Lyssica scribbled their names in the register. "We're trying to race it back to Garadenya. Spread the word about the weather amongst the guards, would you, Brom?"

"Absolutely, my lady." Brom casually saluted them as they went outside again.

Kynthcat flanked her on the short path to the postern exit but pulled ahead as Lozito saw them coming and opened the small gate. *'The dolt didn't even check outside! Anything could be waiting out there.'* He growled. *'Poorly trained.'*

Ensuring he was between Lyssica and the exit, Kynthcat opened his mouth, tasting the air as he listened intently. Slightly mollified when he sensed no danger, he eased forward until they could do a visual check of the road outside. When he was satisfied all was as it should be, he paced through the opening, waiting for Lyssica to finish her chat with Lozito.

Crossing the road to the forest and the now familiar narrow path, they moved in single file with Kynthcat leading, senses on full alert. By now, they knew which way took them to Ostara's circle and when they reached it, Lyssica wasted no time. She spun around the perimeter, breaking into immediate, low-voiced song as she moved though the impromptu steps of her power dance.

Kynthcat shadowed her; he'd no wish to be distant if trouble found them. Opening his senses wide, he kept one eye on her and another on their surroundings. Even not paying full attention, he couldn't help responding to her ceremony, as he had since the first day. It was like she opened a bag and started flinging handfuls of love, well-being and reassurance for all the animals and plants. The feeling was amazing and he revelled in it. Not only the power she held, but that it came from her, although he wished he could work out why it made him want to pounce on her and made him putty in her hands.

But the way it made him feel … No wonder so many varieties of fauna flocked here for the 'hands-on' part of Lyssica's duties.

A variety of animals were now flowing around him on their way to Lyssica. The creatures showed no fear of Kynthcat's large form, hadn't even on the first day, despite his fangs, claws and the twisted twin horns on his skull. He was peripherally pleased that none of the smaller creatures showed any fear of Kynthcat. Perhaps some of Lyssica's scent lingered in his fur? And why did he like that idea so much?

Finally, his circuit brought him to a clear section stretching several ells back from the Ostara Circle until it reached two gnarled bushes. The space was devoid of animal presence. He cocked his head, studying the area. What was different about it? The branches of the bushes were spindly, and what was left of the leaves drooped in an unhealthy manner. As he stared at the bushes, he started to notice the emanations of an icy-blue glow. He paced closer, uneasiness growing.

Crouching down to lie flat, he twisted his huge head sideways to peer under the lowest branches of one bush. Wrapped around the base of the trunk was a solid looking, frosty blue growth. When he checked, the second bush revealed the same stuff. The attachments glowed with an ugly, unwholesome light and looked tight enough to strangle. In addition, glowing blue filaments snaked out of the parasitic mass, stretching glacial claws up the trunks. Extending a paw, he prodded at the blue mass with a claw tip. Quick as lightning, a frigid tendril extruded from the growth, darting at his paw. He snatched it back. The thread barely brushed his fur, but still caused a brief painful jolt of frozen electricity. Every hair on his paw stood on end. Oh, hell, no. This wasn't good.

Shaking his paw out, he turned his head in Lyssica's direction and emitted a low coughing roar. She and the group of animals with her all looked up. Lyssica's brows rose. Using the afflicted paw, he beckoned.

He took another look under the attack bush as he waited. The vicious icy tendril was still poised, waving around as if searching for what had annoyed it. Without any prompts from him, Lyssica lowered herself to the ground.

"By my Goddess! What is that abomination? It's killing these bushes, but it looks sort of frosty." She glanced at him. "Did you touch it? Is that why it's acting defensive?" He rumbled an assent, shaking his paw. "Let me see." She clasped both hands around it, inspected the singed spot, then sang softly, aiming her words into the fur. The goddess power flowed into his paw through her hands. It was augmented by her song and immediately eased the cold ache.

He leaned in and nuzzled her cheek. She smiled, then turned

her attention back to the tree, smile fading. Wearing an expression of determination, Lyssica re-commenced singing, the words louder and more forceful. She held her hands, palms out, focusing on the strangling cankers. The malignant bulges shivered. Higher up in the bushes, the icy-blue shimmer stuttered and began to fade. Next the tips of the reaching tendrils shrank back towards the main swelling until the serpentine strands had pulled back completely.

Lyssica kept singing until the lumps were reduced to tiny nodules and then even those were gone. Still she sung, lowering her hands to focus on the roots. The ground quivered a little, but slowly settled and stilled. Lyssica changed her song and alternated moving her hands between the roots and back to the trunks of the bushes. Before long the plants were vibrant and healthy, getting even more so when Lyssica touched them. When she stopped singing and eased back, she was mobbed by little furry creatures, who keened in delight as she cuddled and stroked them all.

He watched in awe. She was simply amazing. He could come up with no other appropriate words. Although, gorgeous also came to mind when he thought of her.

CHAPTER NINE

LYSSICA

"The forest sprawls over a large tract of land and we've patrolled widely." Lyssica frowned, her gaze drifting between tree trunks, hands on hips. "I doubt it's a coincidence that these killer growths are focused only in the area between Papillion and Garadenya."

Beside her, Kynthcat snorted. His mouth opened, his tongue curling out to taste the ether. "Mmroww."

Clutching a handful of fluffy mane, Lyssica grinned. "I can't get over you being able to 'taste' their smell – like rotten blueberries, you said?" She grimaced. "Nasty."

He worked his tongue, then hissed. "Gssst." In the six weeks since they'd found the first growth, there'd been at least one every day and, in a wonderful stroke of luck, his air-tasting sense traced them with unerring accuracy.

She tilted her head. "Can you sense any more infestations? Or any signs of the devil-rabbit?" He shook his head, huge mane flopping from side to side. "Good." She eyed the building clouds. "At least it's not snowing, so far." Blizzards, sleet and snowfall had intensified over the Moon of Juberd and continued into the Moon of Julary.

Winter had set in with a vengeance. An occasional weak, sunny day reared its head, but the temperature had dropped to freezing and stayed there. The sky was mostly covered in either stark white or gloomy grey cloud. She and Emryn continued the daily routine they'd begun as best they could. The harshness of the weather resulted in Lyssica rarely being able to fly; her wings were too delicate for strong winds and didn't function once wet, but after six weeks, their pattern of dividing the day between Garadenya, Papillion and the forest was well set.

"Rrow." Kynthcat rumbled deep in his chest as he nudged her out of her revery. She turned as he dropped to lie flat.

"Yes, you're right." She swung her leg over his back and settled, tucking her feet around his rib cage and grasping strands of his mane in both fists. Surging to his feet, he loped towards the Rubiconia River, threading between the trees, only stopping every now and then to re-test the air.

Riding comfortably, Lyssica sang, her words tiny pieces of power which the breeze of their passage scattered through the forest like seeds on the wind. She loved this benefit of Emryn and Kynthcat's company. In past winters, spreading her Ostara given power had relied on very loud vocals and how far she could travel in the wintry conditions. Only on a good day was she able to use her wings.

Beneath her, the muscles of Kynthcat's powerfully moving frame bunched and released. She revelled in it. His musky scent of rain-soaked forest drifted up to her, something she now associated with safety. Yes, he was guarding her, but, to her delight, he'd also been actively assisting in her work. She'd never guessed how much she'd enjoy having someone's wholehearted support. She'd come to rely on him a lot in her Handmaidenly duties.

Who was she kidding? She didn't just rely on him for that. She adored *him*. Longed for this to continue. Was there any way she could get him to stay on after the end of the Tri-moon program? She sighed. Naturally he'd have a life, commitments within his pack, so he probably wasn't interested in a chance-met female. Especially one with hang-ups like hers.

She nosedived, getting a face full of fluffy mane as Kynthcat skidded to a halt. "Ouch!" Under her legs, his ribs vibrated, a continuous snarl rumbling from his muzzle. Spitting out a mouthful of hair, she shoved to a sitting position and blinked, focusing between his outward curled horns to see what had upset him.

"Is that a spider's web? It's huge. I've not seen anything like it before." Lyssica stared as she gingerly touched her squashed nose. "I can't see it properly." She slid from Kynthcat's back, intending to approach, but he was a solid wall between her and the over-sized web. "Hey, you lump of rock! Move it." She poked him in the ribs, expecting him to step aside. Instead, he growled at her, not only continuing to block her from reaching the unusual web but nudging her further away. She sighed.

"Okay, I know it's likely dangerous. I know you're protecting me, but I have a job to do and this is part of it. You know that too, Emryn." His snarl faded. He looked at the strange web again, then hissed. But he eased to one side so she could approach where it extended between two tree trunks.

From several paces away, solid strands of shiny white crystal shaped a larger than normal open weave, spiralling inward like a funnel. It was interconnected by spokes to keep the shape in one roughly circular piece – quite weblike – but it radiated coldness, which was odd. The funnel centre contained an obscuring density. Was something there?

Lyssica stepped closer, craning her neck for a better look. The structure rippled, energy surged and—

Kynthcat roared. He lunged, hitting the back of her knees, throwing her off balance. A second blow hit the side of her neck and waves of painful cold seared her flesh, the agony increasing second by second. Something clung to her skin. Tightened and dug in.

She gasped, gloved fingers rising to claw at the spot. "It hurts, it burns!"

Kynthcat's snarling face eclipsed the surrounding forest. Time slowed. A paw rose, curving to smack her; she was already screaming as his massive paw, sharp claws fully extended, obscured her vision. The icy wind of their passing chilled her face, fur brushed her flesh, then, wicked claws dug into her neck – she jerked under the impact. Flesh tore and liquid trickled, a macabre tickling sensation. Why was this happening? The blazing torment at her throat intensified. She shrieked her pain, fear and betrayal as—

He ripped her throat out.

Crack, crack, crack! Shards of crystal sprayed as Kynthcat's paw completed its arc. Iridescent crystalline chunks splintered crisply as they hit the ground and cartwheeled across the uneven terrain. The intense cold searing her neck vanished, leaving a deep stinging ache.

Lyssica crumpled; the forest floor, heavy and solid, whacked her in the back. The sky whirled above her in sickening swirls of white and grey. A cold wetness smooshed against her neck, smothering the burning sensation until it diminished to a dull throb. Staring, senses reeling, her every breath strained and torturous, she could only blink mindlessly when the heavens were blotted out by a blur of deep brown. Strands of fur fell softly against her cheek. A warm dampness began to gently brush at her tortured throat. Again and again the soft stroke returned, soothing scraped skin, dulling the sting of pain and somehow … somehow … calming her panic. Her hands reached blindly and she clasped silky fur between her fingertips, felt it tickling gently under her palms.

"Emryn?" Screaming had reduced her voice to a hoarse whisper. Every breath rasped viciously in her chest and throat, her vision was compromised, but she recognised the feel of his fur.

And he was tending her, which meant ... He hadn't torn her neck open? Understanding washed over her. Relief followed hard on its heels. No, of course he hadn't; he'd saved her.

His low growl suddenly became words. "Some guard I am! I know you have to do your work, but now you're wounded and I can't stand—"

Lyssica closed her fingers in his hair and jerked him down. Her lips mashed into his, the kiss a rough, slightly off-centre joining which he squirmed to correct. His mouth tasted as delectable as his alluring scent suggested. Strong arms wormed beneath her, firmed, then she was raised, pulled against him. Sensations swamped – the touch of his mouth, the feel of his cradling arms, her hands in his hair – those were her only points of reference. His response was ardent, his lips as eager as hers. She licked her tongue against his upper lip, into his suddenly open mouth and his tongue surged to join, to twine with her own. It was wonderful. It was delicious.

It was crazy.

Pulling away, Lyssica turned her head and rested it against his cheek. Her neck stung and she swallowed heavily, wishing she could ignore the pain. She drew a breath and – Emryn's delicious scent was strong in her nostrils, helping her to re-image the kiss in her mind, bask in the return of being sexually attracted to another; something she'd never thought to enjoy again after the bitter pain left by—

"Lyssica? Tell me you're okay!" He peppered the top of her ear with tiny kisses.

Her voice was tremulous. "I-I think so. By the Goddess, what was that? It feels like I have a very painful sunburn." She was tilted away from him slightly and couldn't help her brittle murmur of protest. "N-nooo."

"It's okay, I just need to look at the wound." His husky reassurance calmed her. "How does it feel."

"Not as bad as it did, thank goodness. Whatever action you took and the substances you put on it were tremendously effective." Her swallow was painful. "I'm sorry, but I thought you were going to kill me. I saw your fangs then your claws and—"

"Little fool." The humour in his voice took the barb from his words. "I was doing my job, saving you."

"Your job?" She was drooling over him and he saw her as a duty? The warmth inside her was suddenly chill. "Oh, of course. My apologies. Your job, I—"

"Stop." His arms tightened. "Let's be clear before your get any crack-brained ideas. *You* are not a job, but I was given the job of keeping *you* safe. There is a huge contrast between the two and I'll not have you confused about it. Okay?"

"I … yes, okay."

He kissed her ear again. "Do you understand the difference? I want to be sure."

She started to nod; the sting stopped her. "I do see the distinction." But she wasn't certain where it took them. "Ah, what exactly happened?"

He snorted. "That web thing is a weapon. I sensed it was dangerous, but I didn't know what it would do. Kynthcat can't talk so we were pushing you away, but you persisted and sprung the thing's trap. I bumped you aside, but too late to avoid it completely. A sort of web thingy ejected at high speed, landed on your neck, and was digging into your flesh when I hooked it away. That action also smashed it to pieces – peeled away from your body it became hard and crystalline – but if I hadn't pushed you when I did, it would have landed on your face."

Shuddering at the thought, Lyssica's fingers came up to feel her wound.

"No touching. The vile thing's caused a nasty burn and torn your skin with that ugly web."

"Which I triggered with my proximity."

"The hazards of the profession, I guess. But ..." He tilted her chin up, forcing her to stare at the cosmos again. "Even though it goes against my protective nature, I won't second-guess your skills. I know we're still learning the best ways to work together."

82

His lips twisted. "Mistakes always happen when partners are still learning. Neither of us knew *that* was going to attack whatever came near it. However—"

It was her turn to snort. "However. Yeah, I should have been more careful. Approaching from the front? What was I thinking?"

"You were thinking to investigate an anomaly in your forest. We both made a mistake. You approaching it head on; me not recognising the level of the danger. But we live and learn. This time, we're fortunate you're not seriously injured." His fingers gently turned her jaw from side to side. "Pain level out of ten?"

She grimaced. "About four. How'd you help me? Was the cold stuff snow?"

"Yeah. After I ripped it from your neck and shattered it, I packed on snow to ease the pain, but it's time to return to Garadenya and get some burn salve on it. Are you okay to travel?"

She tilted her head, met his silvery-grey gaze. "Only snow? What was the soft repetitive drag?"

His eyebrows rose. "Did it hurt?"

"No, no, no." She smiled weakly. "It really helped."

He nodded. "Good. Kynthcat was frantic – it was his tongue. He feels better for helping and now, I'd better change back so we can get moving."

"Change back?" Great goddess! They were talking and cuddling and they'd kissed and, and he was not able to do any of that as Kynthcat. Which meant … "Ohmygoddess! You're naked! That's not your leg I can feel – or maybe it is! Is that your leg? Please tell me it's your leg!" She was on her feet, with her back to him without even realising she'd leapt from his lap.

His uncontrollable laughter suddenly became the chuffing of a highly amused Kynthcat. She turned around to see him rolling on the ground, paws mirthfully batting the air.

Glaring, Lyssica snatched up a fallen, but still leafy, branchlet and swatted him across the flank.

CHAPTER TEN

EMRYN

"*J* came across them several times, when hunting rogue Ice-trolls." Dario stopped pacing to eye them grimly. "You ran afoul of a Vulpiawolf attack-web."

Scrubbing his head tiredly, Emryn sighed. "Well, cat-crap."

Lyssica frowned. "Vulpiawolves? In our forest? I don't know much about them."

Emryn grimaced. "I'm from warm lands and they thrive in wintry conditions, so I have never come across any before. But I have heard of them. They're vicious apparently."

Picking up his whisky-nectar, Dario cradled the beaker between his palms. "Be glad you've not met up with them – they *are* vicious. They're also malicious and often destructive. The pack has probably come down from the Northern Ice Wastes." He took a sip. "But what would have drawn them here?"

Helping herself to a cookie from the tray on the table, Lyssica contemplated the cholickalate chips. "What do they look like? I need to be able to recognise them." She bit into the cookie. "Mmm."

Emryn was overcome with a sudden need for his own cookie. Dario continued as he sat next to Zhulija. "Their fur is a light greenish grey, but spiky rather than soft. They're spotted with the same green through a darker grey fur on their backs, although their fur coats only cover their body. Their legs are smooth, having dark grey skin speckled with small pale green oval marks. Their paws are five-clawed. Add to that narrow-pointed muzzles and ears, and a spike-furred tail with barbed tip, and you can't mistake them for any other creature."

Still contemplating the cookies, Emryn made a snap decision and snatched two before dropping into a comfortable chair. "And the attack-webs? Do you know how they're constructed? We saw lots of them after Lyssica recovered. She smashed them, from the side, with a club while Kynthcat flung whatever his claws could scoop. We disarmed as many as we found."

Zhulija stirred. "My avalanche power of flinging objects from a distance would be useful."

"Yes, as we unfortunately discovered, the web darts are set off by the target's nearness." Emryn met Lyssica's gaze. "We're going to have to do a daily sweep."

Lyssica winced. "Any idea how the Vulpiawolves create the stuff?"

Dario drew Zhulija closer. "As far as I know, the web stuff somehow extrudes from their claws as a soft substance, before hardening to ice. The claws are thick and hollow, like a tube. They also use the stuff like rope, to bind things, without the missile centre, of course."

Emryn frowned. "It broke easily."

"Binding-web ice is much thicker and stronger than attack-web." Dario reached for a cookie and handed it to Zhulija, before taking another and eyeing it in a predatory manner. "Plus Vulpia-wolves hunt in packs."

Lyssica's eyes widened. "So multiple Vulpiawolves could bind you at the same time. That's bad. I wonder if the ice burns like the dart from the attack-web." She fingered her bandage-wrapped neck, causing Emryn to stiffen, while Kynthcat hissed and paced; he hated that she'd been in pain. Although, she was more relaxed since Zhulija had treated the wound with healing salve, applied a bandage and given her a pain-relieving herbal draught.

Dario swallowed a mouthful of cookie. "It all burns, but with a cold burn because it's ice."

Emryn lifted his beaker of whisky-nectar, swirling the liquid. "Do you think they're in league with the Bodach? Another one of his tools like the devil-rabbit?"

Lyssica nodded. "I wondered about that; the Bodach is cunning."

Dario exhaled. "I'm forced to agree. It would be a huge coincidence and we all know there's no such thing."

Zhulija nodded. "Yes, we've endured the devil-rabbit as the Bodach's messenger, the cancerous blue plant growths and now the Vulpia-webs, courtesy of a probable invasion of Vulpiawolves. What's next?"

Lyssica met her sister's gaze. "I've been thinking about that. As a consort to the Goddess of Winter, he has a lot of choice and control. He can call on anything with a cold vibration or winter-link."

Zhulija nodded. "Then these events are not just random bad luck. If we can figure out why it's happening, we may gain clues on what to expect and how to counter it."

"Okay." Emryn gestured with half a cookie. "Actions are usually based on want or need. So, what's the Bodach seeking?"

Brows wrinkled, Lyssica nibbled a cholickalate chunk. "To answer that, we'll summarise what we know of him. First, he's consorted to the Goddess of Cold and Wind."

Zhulija pleated her skirt with restless fingers. "True, but is he the alpha in their relationship?"

"I doubt it." Lyssica shook crumbs onto her plate. "Because, although she's also known as the Queen of Winter, he's never been called King."

Zhulija nodded. "So maybe he wants to be King of Winter? What else do we know?"

Contemplating the cookie tray, Emryn rubbed his jaw. "The

myths state he likes to play tricks on others for his own amusement. They're reputed to not always be pleasant tricks." His hand hovered over the tray. "Sending a devil-rabbit, killing Lord Roland and exploding his body is proof of that." He succumbed to the cookie temptation and bit into another one.

Dario placed his whisky-nectar glass on the table. "He did say he hoped Lyssica, as Ostara's representative, enjoyed the show, but I fail to see killing as a fun activity, unless you're insane." He tapped the glass. "Lyss, I recall you saying that the devil-rabbit may have been an assumed body too?"

"Yes." She licked a streak of cholickalate from her lower lip; Emryn shifted in his chair, trying to ignore suddenly tight pants. "I was thinking the rabbit thing could have *been* the Bodach."

Dario frowned. "It spoke as if it wasn't. It said: 'The Bodach hopes you enjoyed the show.' Or something similar, which indicates it wasn't the Bodach."

"Ye-esss." Lyssica reached for her teacup. "But it wouldn't be the first time a being has referred to themself in the third person."

"It's a possibility." Emryn tilted his head, still riveted on Lyssica's pink mouth. He cleared his throat, suppressed memories of their explosive kiss. "But, one would assume, since the Bodach is her consort, the Cailleach knows what he's up to."

Zhulija and Lyssica met each other's eyes and broke into laughter.

Emryn's brows arched. "What's so funny?"

Lyssica shook her head. "Just because a couple is consorted doesn't mean they know every little thing about their partner or what they do. Zhu and I were thinking about Maman and Papan in that light." Fingertips rising to cover her lips, she chuckled again. "Nope, just nope."

Even Dario was grinning. "When you take a mate Emryn, you'll see the funny side of that comment too."

"Alright." Emryn's hands turned palm out. "So, the Cailleach may not know what her consort is doing?"

Lyssica's mouth thinned. "That's more than likely."

Zhulija leaned forward. "Is that deliberate? Is he hiding something from her?"

Dario pursed his lips. "Or trying to achieve something without her knowledge?"

Lyssica nodded. "Yes, good point! Something like a present, or a surprise? Despite his sly nature, he is rumoured to adore her."

Emryn put his glass down. "I like that idea. He's been her consort for eons and there's never been rumours about him wanting to be King."

"That's true." Dario wagged a finger. "However, his dissatisfaction could have been building for a long time."

"Maybe." Emryn spread his hands. "But, not everyone wants to be in charge; some of us are content to back our leader, as I'm currently doing for Lyssica." *'And loving it.'*

"Hmm." Dario cupped Zhulija's shoulder and pulled her back into the circle of his arm. "Your pack life gives you a uniquely helpful viewpoint, Emryn. If we continue the line of thought of the Bodach not aiming to be alpha, then, we can accept the possibility he's doing something for the Cailleach's benefit. Even if she's in the dark."

"I wish I could communicate with Ostara." Lyssica ran a hand through her hair fretfully. "She could speak to the Cailleach and this business would be sorted very quickly."

Zhulija stared. "Could the block be deliberate?"

"To stop me bringing in Ostara? You could be right." Lyssica fanned her hands in frustration. "But whether it's deliberate or not, I still can't get through to her, which means I'm on my own – sorry, *we're* on our own."

Zhulija's brow wrinkled. "If you can't call for help, the Bodach has longer to achieve his purpose, doesn't he?"

Emryn's mouth twisted. "Which means he assumes his powers are stronger than those you possess, Lyssica."

She sighed. "They most likely are. After all, he's consort to a goddess while I'm merely Handmaiden of one."

Dario pointed. "Don't sell yourself short Lyssica Aphiski. From what both Zhu and Emryn say, you've quite amazing abilities. Admit he's more powerful and you're all but conceding defeat. Whatever he's up to, we can't afford to lose and you're our best hope."

Lyssica flung up her hands. "Wow! Way to stack the pressure on! It's winter, which is their season, so he's super strong. I wield spring power and it's not spring, so I'm weaker."

"But winter is *always* vanquished by spring." Emryn tossed in. "You – we – can't lose."

"Thank goodness!" Zhulija shivered. "Can you imagine if it was always winter?"

An electric silence filled the room as they all stared at her.

"Oh!" Lyssica's hands flew to her mouth.

"That's it!" Emryn was on his feet. "That's got to be it."

Dario hugged his consort. "You're brilliant sweetheart! Eternal winter, tied up in a bow from the Bodach to his mate. What better gift is there?"

Escorting Lyssica through the halls of Garadenya Fortress to their shared suite, Emryn's eyes were riveted to Lyssica's svelte form. His mouth watered and his cock thickened. Inside him, fur ruffled and claws jabbed; Kynthcat prowled. *'Want her.'*

'So you keep saying.'

'You do too. Your prick on alert.'

Emryn huffed. *'She's gorgeous, but it's not possible.'*

Pausing in the doorway, Lyssica glanced at him. "Something wrong?"

He summoned a grin. "Just tired. Today was gruelling."

His cat persisted. *'She ours.'*

'We're only visiting for three moons!'

'Take her home with us.' Cat logic. Simple and direct.

Emryn massaged his forehead. *'We can't do that! Her job is a critical part of her make-up.'*

A fur driven shrug. *'We stay here then. It work well. Fulfil our directive to create connections between shifter tribes and outsider Fae.'*

'But we're bound to the pack! I can't ... we need ... you ... they'd never ... it's not...'

A warm palm touched his cheek. Jerked from his pointless pronoun babbling, he peered between his cupped fingers, gulping as he registered the tender expression on Lyssica's face. *'There! See?'* A very smug Kynthcat preened his whiskers. *'She adore us as a mate should.'*

'Mate?!' A tide of red seeped up his neck and a deep gurgling sound choked him. His desperately seeking hand hit the nearby wall in direct response to the dizziness flooding him. He fought it, denied Kynthcat's instincts. *'What in time-sands are you talking about?'*

'You a silly kitbabe. Not know mate even when she loves on us. You want a Seer reading. Pah!' A paw waved dismissively. *'Who needs Seer when truth and our very own beauty, luscious and ripe in our face?'*

'You're wrong! She can't possibly be our mate. She's not changeling ...'

"Emryn?" Lyssica's eyebrows furrowed. "Are you alright?"

"Ah, ah, yes." He fought for words. "Nothing a good night's rest won't cure."

Kynthcat lay down and put both paws over his eyes. *'I in error. You not just a silly kitbabe, you a scared, silly, kitbabe dummy.'*

'You can take a long walk off a short time-sand pier!'

Kynthcat chuffed his mirth. *'Only problem with that, if I do what you say, I take you with me, scaredy kitbabe!'*

Staring up at him, brows still creased, Lyssica patted his cheek. "You're probably right, but there's something I'd like to discuss – if you're not too tired?" Her mouth quirked hopefully. "I could give your neck a massage. If that would help?"

Kynthcat snorted. *'Not neck muscles he want massaged, Lyss-mate.'*

"Um. Massage? Ah, maybe." Emryn swallowed convulsively, ignoring Kynthcat. "You're correct though, we do need to talk about ... Ah ... About things, yeah things ..."

"Good." Grasping his hand, Lyssica towed Emryn into the

sitting room of their suite. She dropped to sit on the sofa he would be opening into a bed later, as he had every night since they'd taken up residence. She still held his hand, so he'd little choice but to sink down near her, unless he pulled his hand free and moved further away. *That* would be extremely juvenile and he wasn't a child, so he sat, trying to hide how much he wanted to pounce on her.

"Well." He scraped the palm of his free hand up and down his thigh. "Here we are."

"Yes." Lyssica twisted to face him, then tilted her head. "Is there something wrong with your hand?"

"My hand?" He lifted the offending limb and stared at it. "Er, I think it might be itchy. Yes! That's right. It's itchy."

She peered at him. "You seem uncomfortable. What is it?"

"Um." He shrugged, glanced around for inspiration. "Wow, when did it get so dark? I must have missed that. How about I light the lamps? I'll just do that, yeah?" As a shape shifter, he had excellent night vision, but she wouldn't know that. He half rose from the sofa, but her firm tug on his captured hand aborted the action. Still loath to pull free of her grip, Emryn cast her a desperate glance.

She smiled ruefully. "Looks like I need to apologise."

He gawked. "Apologise? For what?"

"You're suddenly uncomfortable with me." Her hands clasped together, gripping his hand firmly between her palms. "The only difference is, I kissed you today. I'm not sorry, but I'll apologise if it helps."

One swift indrawn breath and he planted himself firmly on the sofa, face close to hers. "Apology rejected, Lyssica. My problem, my discomfort, directly relates to my aching need for more of your kisses."

"Oh!" Heat flooded her cheeks. "In that case, what's stopping – mmf—"

Emryn's mouth slid across hers, effectively muffling the rest of her sentence.

CHAPTER ELEVEN

LYSSICA

*L*yssica's hands emptied as Emryn pulled from her grasp, but his palms returned to cup her cheeks, slide into her hair. His lips twisted deliciously against hers, nipping, nibbling, enticing ... She opened her mouth on a gasp allowing his tongue to surge inside, deepening their connection and over-whelming her with his decadently spicy essence. After the disaster that had brought her party years to a brutal close, she'd never expected to desire a male ever again – but here she was, falling into a haze of need. The combination of his musky, fresh rain scent, the caress of his seductive lips and hands and the glide of his tongue combining to befuddle her senses.

His mouth eased from hers, spread kisses along her jaw. You're adorable Lyssica." His voice rumbled against the side of her neck, just below her ear, before his seeking lips enveloped her ear lobe, sucking and licking, until she quaked with fiery arousal.

Her head tipped back, the pleasure gifted by Emryn's touch chasing away the lingering taint of her darkest memories. The demons which had haunted her for so many years were as nothing in the face of his honest passion, the wild strength of him buoying her confidence until she reached out blindly, shaping the muscles of his chest through the thin cloth of his shirt. "Need skin."

Leaning away, Emryn fisted the back of his top and hauled it over his head. Lyssica's eager fingers travelled over his pectoral muscles, massaging and stroking the taut leaf-brown skin, then his talented lips found hers, his tongue licking the seam of her mouth. The kiss became open-mouthed, their eager tongues seeking, exploring, wrestling, before his mouth moved to spread kisses along her jaw.

She petted up and over his shoulders, tugging him closer so their chests rubbed together in an attempt to assuage the tingling fullness swamping her breasts. "Oh, yes."

"Better skin to skin." Emryn's lips tickled the corner of her mouth. "Raise your hands." Lyssica did so, cloth rustled as her top was swept off over her head and eased around her wings. He licked his lips, eyes a lazy, sexy, burning brand as they roved, until her nipples hardened, drawing his focus. She basked in his molten silver gaze as it became riveted on her full breasts, which thrust high and firm against their gauzy breast-band. His head lowered, mouth nipping and kissing, tongue wetting both her breast-band and the aching nubs the cloth concealed.

"Oh." Her fingertips shaped claws, dug into his heavily muscled chest.

"Keep doing that!" The expulsion of hot breath as he gasped was a further delight to her breasts. They ached, they needed ... She rubbed them across his face, arched to push one point against his lips. His mouth opened, fusing hotly around the wanting pertness. Palms stroked up her body, feathered across her other impatient nipple. Fingers caressed, gathered the damp fabric of her breast-band to rub to-and-fro across the peak. Pleasure expanded, shot in a direct line to her groin where fire bloomed and dampness grew.

"Emrynnnn ..." Lyssica's voice sighed out of her; a direct contrast to the urgent raising of her hips as they sought, searched

... there! A warm hard bulge against her thigh. Wrong place. She twisted, wriggled, trying for a better connection.

"Lyss?" Her lover raised his head slightly, eyes like pools of silvery lava. So enticing, but he'd paused in his ministrations to both breasts and that wouldn't do. Not at all.

Surging forward, her arms wrapping around his neck, body sandwiching his, she shoved. Emryn's eyes widened as he fell backward into the sofa, Lyssica riding him all the way. Knees either side of his hips, skirts frothing around her, she squirmed to connect the firm ridge in his pants with the hot, heavy aching desire between her thighs. Achieving her goal, she writhed and rubbed against him, almost sobbing as the fire blossomed to an inferno of want, of need.

It was a revelation she'd never expected to experience. And she wasn't going to let it disappear before she'd gotten her chance to fully appreciate their togetherness. Her hands reached for his, brought palms back to aching breasts.

"This." Emryn wrestled with the breast band. "Off!" There was a ripping sound, then cool air bathed her upper body. He stroked up from her waist, cupped her heated, heavy breasts. "Time sands! You're so exquisite, my Lyss." His hands shaped, kneaded. Fingers plucked gently.

The sight of her firm mounds filling Emryn's hands, the feel of those hands against her straining bosom added fuel to the fire of desire. Lyssica squirmed against his groin, the action and the feelings it engendered drawing sounds of pleasure from them both. "I need you, Emryn. I can't go another day watching and wanting ..."

His chuckle was hoarse. "Not just me then. You've bewitched me from the very first. Best thing you did was fall into my arms. Only ..." He hesitated. "I can't make any promises, Lyss. When the program is over, I must return home to my pack." Her hips undulated against him, her mouth falling open at the intense pleasure.

Words dropped from ruby lips. "I want you, Emryn. This is for me and I want you. The future can take care of itself."

He shuddered beneath her and grasped her hips. "Then, I'm yours, love. Take what you want, give us what we both need."

His smile radiated all the way to the glory of her femininity, making it pulse with desire. "Pants." Her fingers scrabbled at his belt, unlatching it, then the fastenings of his trousers fell victim to her intent. "Lift." He obeyed and she pulled his pants down past his thighs.

"Now you." Stretching, he raised her skirts, holding them while she rose to her knees, shoved her tights down over her bottom, then sat sideways and twisted to yank them off completely. His hands were there, guiding her back over his thighs, as eager as she for their joining.

Lyssica clasped fingers around his rigid length. "Look at you! So long and thick." She ran fingers down to his balls and back, traced the contours of the swollen head, brought her fingers to her lips, slick with his pre-cum. "I'm burning for you, Emryn."

His words were a husky murmur. "I'm clean. Are you protected? Because I have nothing with me. Although, shifters can only get their mates pregnant, so there's no worry about that."

"Yes. Clean and protected, a side perk of my goddess power."

He frowned. "I thought one of Ostara's abilities was fertility?"

She grinned, still caressing him. "Two sides of the same coin. All's well."

"Good." His forefinger circled a nipple, repeated the action on the other before pulling her close, lashing the first one with his tongue. The action lodged the hot stiffness of his cock firmly between her thighs until it nestled against her pubes, flexed hungrily against her mons.

"Oh, oh, oh, yes!" She lifted slightly, easing her opening back and forth over his unyielding shaft. She was willing putty in his hands as he coaxed her up, then lowered her to engulf his rod in the depths of her wet channel. Pushing high and deep, he filled and stretched her in a tumult of blissful delight. Her sigh mirrored his gasp, both of them stilling as they adjusted to their intimate connection.

95

Emryn's fingers feathered delightfully on her skin. "You okay, my Lyss?"

Nodding joyfully, Lyssica kissed him. "You feel sooo wonderful Emryn." Her movement caused a delicious friction where they were joined, eliciting indrawn breaths. Seeking to repeat the feeling, Lyssica swivelled her hips; Emryn lunged to meet her, pressing and thrusting. Eyes locked, cheeks flushed, panting and entwined, they kept loving until the tiny muscles in Lyssica's passage began to flutter and quake.

"Shite yes!" Emryn's mutter combined with her wail of gratification; her climax milking him to fulfilment. Clutching each other, they shook and shuddered until Lyssica collapsed against his sweaty chest with a huge sigh. Snuggling her cheek against his skin, unable to muster enough strength to move, she revelled in the sensations of Emryn's warm hands stroking her back.

A little later, he pulled a blanket from the back of the sofa to cover them, before wrapping his arms around her. Warm and cosy, they drifted off to sleep.

They stirred twice more during the dark hours, to reach and caress and love again. Each time was equally as wonderful as their first joining.

Now, morning light filtered in through the window and Lyssica studied Emryn's sleeping face, licking her lips as she recalled the night's pleasures.

Will I ever get enough of him? Her heart said no.

A large hand began to stroke her spine, something he apparently enjoyed – as did she. One eye opened, peered lazily at her. "Lyssica, my sweet. I doubt I'll tire of looking at you under any circumstances; you're everything I've always wanted. I'd love us to be able to stay here forever, but unfortunately, the day calls."

Regret twisted her mouth. "Duties and responsibilities. Yep, still there waiting for us." She eased away. "I call first dibs on the shower."

He tilted his head, batted his eyelids. "We could share ..." Grinned as she started to giggle, but the grin faded and his eyes glazed over as her breasts jiggled enticingly. Lyssica gasped as his hand feathered up her body to stroke ...

The shower happened.

Eventually.

A very long shower.

After their mutual satisfaction was achieved and both were washed, Emryn dried and dressed quickly. "Must go, sweeting. I'm late meeting Dario."

She winked. "I know – not sorry."

He kissed her. The press of his lips was meant to be brief, but Lyssica threw herself into the embrace and he was seduced into lingering for several scorching moments. "Unh." His eyes were closed as he drew back and, when they flicked open to pin her in smouldering silver whirlpools, his voice emerged a growl. "Hold that thought for later, beloved." This time his mouth found her cheek, her forehead and her other cheek, before he rushed out the doorway of their suite and was gone.

Sighing happily, Lyssica finished her morning toilette and left their quarters to join Zhulija in the breakfast room. Her sister was filling a plate from dishes arrayed on the sideboard as Lyssica entered.

Zhulija beamed a welcoming smile. "Good morning, Lyss. Looks like we're all late getting up this morning. Sleep well?"

A heated tide swept up Lyssica's neck into her cheeks. "Oh, um yes. Very well. I feel so rested. A lovely night ..." She trailed off as Zhulija grinned at her knowingly.

"If it was like our night, it probably was lovely. I imagine you're quite sore this morning."

Lyssica's mouth tightened. She busied herself by reaching for a clean plate and inspecting the trays of food. "Not like you're thinking – I wasn't virginal."

Zhulija stilled momentarily, then arranged a slice of toast beside her scrambled eggs and bacon. "Okayyy."

Lyssica's fingers clenched around the plate edges. "Whatever's in your mind right now is probably wrong." She drew a deep breath. "What happened between Emryn and I last night was special because it was the first time the *choice* was mine, and that's how I'm processing it, because—" Goddess! What had she just said? She hadn't meant to ever let anyone know.

The plate in her sister's hands was thrust to the table. Sick horror reflected in Zhulija's expression. "You've been forced – in the past?"

Lyssica shrugged, her mouth twisting bitterly. She didn't really want to talk about it, but then again, she'd already said too much to ever think Zhulija would let it go. She sighed. "I didn't resist." Her eyes were on the patterned wallpaper. "Hard to resist when you've been drugged into unconsciousness."

"Oh Goddess! Lyss! I'm so sorry." Zhulija removed Lyssica's plate from her clenching fingers, set it on the sideboard and drew her sister into a warm hug. "How did I not know this?"

Swallowing heavily, Lyssica burrowed into the affection; for some reason her acceptance of it freed her tongue. "I've never told anyone. It was my own fault; during that stupid rebellious phase when Papan told me I wasn't good enough to learn estate management beside DeMaksim. According to him, young Fae-females only have a place as pampered misses with nothing to do but party and enjoy themselves. So I did, only, some of the folk I met were well-disguised swine."

"Oh, Lyss! It happened more than once?" Moisture filled Zhulija's eyes.

"No, fortunately." Eyeing her sister, Lyssica flung up a hand. "Please, no tears. I've had lots of time to think about what happened and I've come to terms with it. I'd prefer to talk about pleasant matters. Which brings me to last night. It was wonderful and completely consensual and I never thought I'd ever experience anything like it. But now that I have, I'm not sorry."

"Sorry?" Zhulija frowned. "What do you mean?"

Lyssica sighed. "I know our society expects us to remain virginal until we consort, but in reality, that's an outmoded belief and, if it's fair to apply the restriction to females, then it's also applicable to males."

Lowering her arms, Zhulija nodded slowly. "That last is absolutely true, Lyss. Whether we're sexually active, or not, should be our own choice, no matter who we are." She drew back, studied Lyssica. "Even so, it must have been a big deal with Emryn last night after ... I know you said you're not sorry for it but ... Are you certain you're okay? You said you've come to terms with the events – your link, your duties with Ostara, did they help you?"

Lyssica nodded. "My Ostara commitment kept me sane, especially after the incident. I was hurt and confused; first because of Papan and then ... about what happened. But I was the one who went partying, foolishly trusting the folk around me."

"You don't believe you got what you deserved, do you? Because that's—"

"No, no, of course not. That's not what I'm saying. I mean, nobody deserves what happened to me. But I'll admit I've rehashed my lifestyle enough times to see what I should've done differently and to wish I had not gone down the path I did. But please don't think that means my own behaviour excuses that bastard for what he did; what he took from me..." Her hands rose to Zhulija's hips. "There is something I've been meaning to say though, Zhu? And now, I can. I need to apologise for the time I tried making a move on Dario. It was awful. *I* was awful." She spread her hands. "At that point, I was a mess inside, still working through my emotional fallout, thinking all males were untrustworthy and trying to protect you. Poor excuses, I know, but they're all I've got."

Movement in the doorway caught her attention. She turned her head to discover Emryn and Dario frozen in the opening, each of them holding two mugs. Dario wore an expression of angry shock; Emryn's face was filled with murderous fury. Zhulija's hair tickled Lyssica's cheek as she also twisted to eye the Fae-males.

Oh Goddess – had they heard too? From the look on both of their faces, they had; Lyssica firmed her mouth. All of these years she'd kept her secret, but there was no going back now.

CHAPTER TWELVE

EMRYN

"You were sexually assaulted in the past?" Emryn's stomach turned over. "Why didn't you say something? If I'd known I could have made sure you were okay, Lyssica, I would have asked you—" Emryn broke off and thumped the mugs he'd been carrying on the sideboard, heedless of the slopping liquid. He advanced on Lyssica, wanting to touch her, to hug her, to hold her safe, but would she even invite his touch? Had he frightened or traumatised her with his lovemaking? He stared down at Lyssica's beautiful face, feeling helpless and angry on her behalf. "Are you alright?" His mind ran over their activities of the previous night. "We didn't do anything to hurt or upset you?"

Lyssica smiled. "No. No, I enjoyed everything we shared. Thank you for asking but, if you recall, I was with you all the way last night. I would definitely have spoken up if something didn't um, sit well with me."

Approaching slowly, hands also empty, Dario flanked Emryn. "Who did it?"

"Good question." Emryn's voice emerged a growl. "He needs to be taught a lesson and I'd be happy to be the teacher." Inside him Kynthcat raged, pacing to-and-fro, claws digging in with every step, his snarl a low and continuous threat. *'We tear and snap and rend this creature who hurt our female!'*

"I'm not sure giving up his name is wise." Lyssica cocked her head. "I've moved forward, I can't prove anything and he'll deny it."

Emryn's growl deepened. "You think that bothers me? He may deny it all he likes, but as an empath, I feel the truth and as a shapeshifter, I scent it."

Dario briefly tightened his fingers on Lyssica' shoulder. "Lyssica, think about this – you may not be his only victim. A bastard such as this will repeat actions he believes he can get away with. You can't change the past, but what about the future?"

Head rising quickly, Lyssica paled. "Oh! I've never thought about him targeting others." Her fingers covered her lips for a moment, then dropped to her throat. "But he would. Yes, indeed he would."

Zhulija clasped her hand. "So give us a name, Lyss. Help us stop him."

Mouth trembling, Lyssica shook her head. "You're all amazing. I thought maybe … you might blame me given what happened."

Emryn knelt in front of her and took her hands gently, revolted by the thought she had blamed herself in any way for that the actions of an honourless bastard. "No behaviour of yours excuses his. Ever. No male worth his salt would ever take your choices from you."

She looked behind him to see Dario and Zhu nodding in agreement. Zhu bit her lip. "He's right, Lyss. You can't blame yourself. Not even a little bit." There were tears in her sister's eyes.

Dario swallowed. "Please, tell us who it was so we can help you set it a little bit right."

She blinked away tears, sniffing a little before nodding decisively. "Very well. It was Perris Momphiday. Do with the knowledge as you will."

"What?" Zhulija stiffened. "The same one who is Tri-moon guesting at Papillion?"

"Yes."

Suddenly, Emryn vanished, Kynthcat ripping out of him. Roaring, the animal bolted for the door, shedding scraps of clothing as he went.

Lyssica straightened. "Emryn, stop!" Lips taut, Zhulija tightened her comforting grip on her sister's hand.

Dario smiled grimly. "Don't worry, the door's shut and his paws handicap him." He closed in on Emryn, prodding the stymied, snarling Kynthcat in his rump. "Change back! We'll get the bastard, but we'll get him at the right time. Going off like this isn't the answer."

'Rend and gut him!' Kynthcat paced, lips peeled back from his very large, sharp teeth. *'You can't stop me.'* He flicked a wicked glance at Dario then lowered his head, horns aimed at the door.

Zhulija gasped. Lyssica shook her head.

"Emryn, no!"

Baring his own teeth, Dario pointed at Emryn. A small fireball spat and sparked on the tip of his finger. "By Old Mab's teeth and hair! If you start goring my door, I'll singe your hide, Emryn Arion Phengaris! In this place and time, I'm your Alpha and I'm telling you to stand down and change back. *Now!*"

Unable to resist Dario's alpha voiced command, Kynthcat reshaped himself. Naked and furious, Emryn glared, hands digging into hips. "Need to shred him!" His eyes were wild, still glowing with changeling energy.

Dario grabbed a quilt from a nearby chair and flung it at Emryn. "Stop thinking like a predator; it'll do you no favours, right now. And wrap that coverlet around you – I'd much rather Zhu look at and think about my gonads than get an eyeful of yours!"

Muttering, Emryn covered himself. Heat crept up his neck and face. Zhulija emitted a burst of laughter and even Lyssica was grinning. The ladies' reactions also helped to settle all of them. For that alone, he'd forgive Dario's harsh slap of reality. Twisting one hand into his wild hair, he pulled his fingers through the entire length to his shoulder, calming Kynthcat and reining him in. "Sorry. Didn't mean to lose control. Strong emotion feeds our empathic side and extremes of both can trigger uncontrolled savagery in Kynthcat, to the point where neither of us can think straight."

Still chuckling, Zhulija waved one hand. "It's okay, but perhaps you could go and get into fresh clothes?"

Emryn nodded. "Yeah." He shifted his attention to Dario. "Thank you. My apologies." His gaze flickered to Lyssica brows raising.

She smiled tremulously. "Thank you for wanting to defend me."

"Always." He turned and noticed Dario still had the tiny fireball in his hands and was tossing it from one hand to the other. Emryn's eyes narrowed. "Were you really going to zap me?"

"I protect what's mine – even if it is just a door."

"Noted." Emryn finger-combed his hair again.

"Good." The tiny fireball winked out. "Apology accepted." Then Dario grinned. "Go get dressed. We'll make fresh tea and reheat the food."

"I've just realised you used my full name." Emryn lowered his fork to his empty plate, reached for his mug of tea.

Dario grinned, both hands wrapped around his own cup. "That should've told you how serious I was."

Zhulija shook her head, a grin also gracing her lips. "Using a full name is very parentish, my darling Dario. You'll be a great father one day." Pursing his lips, he blew a kiss her way. She pretended to catch it.

Emryn watched Lyssica push some food around her plate. She'd eaten about half of what Zhulija had served her. Inside him, a tail whipped from side to side. *'Our mate still upset. She upset with us?'*

'I keep telling you, she's not our mate.'

Lyssica slanted a glance across the table at him. "I don't think I can manage anymore." Had she heard them?

"Don't then." He stretched a hand out. "I'm sorry if our unruly display added to your distress."

Kynthcat hissed. *'We not unruly.'*

Lyssica dropped her cutlery, accepted the offer of his fingers and twined hers into them. "It's okay, really it is. It showed me I'm not as alone as I thought."

Dario sipped his drink, eyed her shrewdly. "You've never told anyone, you said?"

Lyssica grimaced. "No. I thought it was my trouble to deal with – I wasn't comfortable sharing the details with anyone."

Zhulija rubbed Lyssica's arm. "Not even Maman?"

"No, I thought she'd be ashamed of me. Not about my being molested. But about how I behaved back then – drinking and running with a crowd of people with no thought in their heads other than to have a good time. If I hadn't been with them, getting drunk and behaving rashly, it probably wouldn't have happened."

"Oh Lyss. I'm so sorry you felt like that." Zhulija frowned. "I wish you'd been able to talk to at least one of us. You should be able to." Her frown deepened. "I thought us a close-knit family, but not close enough apparently."

Drumming his fingers on the table, Dario looked at Emryn. "If you're agreeable, we'll skip today's Tri-moon program lesson. You're ahead anyway and we need to plan."

Emryn nodded. "That's fine. Our situation has become increasingly complicated every day since this began. Whenever we go into the forest it's to find more traps and infestations to spike, with no sign of the devil-rabbit or actual sightings of Vulpiawolves. It's frustrating."

Zhulija sighed. "And now there is Perris Momphiday to deal with. Has he bothered you Lyss?"

Lyssica's nose wrinkled. "He's asked for a private meeting several times. I've been ignoring him as best I can; I've no wish to be alone with the creep."

"I should think not!" A growl rattled Emryn's chest. "Bad enough he's at your home, somewhere you should feel safe. Make certain you neither eat nor drink anything he offers." He cocked his head. "I'm assuming that's how he administered the knock-out drug?"

"Yes. A drink." Lyssica massaged her temples. "His turn to pay, he told us and when I began to feel drowsy and unwell, he acted the well-mannered Fae-male and helped me to find a secluded room at the tavern we were partying at. He attacked me, tore my clothes ... I couldn't fight. Probably better that I passed out." She shuddered. "I was so naive."

"I'll kill him." Emryn hissed the words between clenched teeth. His clasp on her hand strengthened.

Lyssica stared, round-eyed. "Kill him? You'd do that?" Her voice emerged a squeak.

Dario leaned back in his chair. "He deserves it, but the action will only get you into serious trouble. We wouldn't want his family to start a vendetta." He pursed his lips. "What we should do is set him up as bait for the devil-rabbit or the Vulpiawolves. Let them do the dirty work, leaving no suspicion on us. Then we've only got to deal with the Bodach and his minions.

Emryn was nodding before Dario had finished speaking. "Great tactics."

An expression of horror crossed Zhulija's face. "You can't just sit there and plot to have someone killed!"

"Why not?" Emryn cocked his head. "We just agreed he's deserving of it."

Dario held up a finger. "Actually, I can. And so can you. The Queens appointed us their representatives. Meting out justice comes within our range of duties; we just have to get him onto Garadenya lands. Our Queens, if they got hold of him, would tear him apart."

"Oh, of course. Justice. That I fully support." Zhulija nodded. "What say you, Lyss?"

She shook her head. "You're wasting your time appealing to me. I've dreamed of shoving a blade into him, but ..." She nibbled her lower lip. "Using him as bait for the Bodach would be very satisfying; and save Emryn having to dirty his hands."

Dario speared her with a look. "That's all perfectly understandable and we do need to draw the Bodach out if we want to defeat him."

Zhulija pursed her lips. "Have you been able to connect with Ostara yet, Lyss?"

Lyssica rubbed the back of her neck. "No, but I'm not giving up, because without her, I don't have a chance."

Emryn squeezed her fingers gently. "You say that because you believe the Bodach more powerful than you."

"He is."

"Not necessarily. Not in the ways that count."

The look she gave him could have melted his heart. "Thank you for your faith in me – it means the world. But even if you're right, it still doesn't guarantee a win against the Bodach."

"What if we resort to trickery?"

Zhulija considered him. "*Is* it possible to trick a trickster?"

"I think so, only because he's so busy running his own scam, he won't expect to have the tables turned."

Dario tapped the side of his mug. "Think of it as attacking him where he least expects it – he'll be vulnerable."

Zhulija frowned. "Does anyone have jurisdiction over the forest between Papillion and Garadenya?"

"Crown land." Dario gestured vaguely. "At a pinch, anyone who is an appointed representative of the Dual Crowns, could exercise their authority there." His mouth formed an 'o' of understanding.

"Exactly. That means us." A sly smile crept over Zhulija's mouth. "Lyss, you should agree to meet with that bastard, Perris. Suggest the forest as neutral ground for the meeting. That's where we'll be waiting, listening as you draw a confession out; then we'll arrest him. He can be strung up as bait for the devil-rabbit. Disposing of that weirdo should draw out the Bodach and ..." She spread her hands.

Emryn grinned. "Oh yes, I like that plan."

"Me too." Dario winked at Zhulija. "Some of my cunning has clearly rubbed off."

Replacing her mug on the table, Lyssica wiped her mouth with a napkin. "Something just occurred to me. Ostara has shared a number of times how much she enjoys having hand-maidenly help. Because she loves what she does, but it's hard work and, essentially, just a job."

Frowning, Zhulija toyed with a fold of the table cloth. "But she's a goddess."

"Who is expected to come back, year after year, doing the same things, over and over." Lyssica steepled her fingers. "She enjoys it, yes and she's worshipped, again yes, but it's because she gives people what they want."

Emryn cocked his head. "So what happens when people don't get what they want? They stop worshipping her? What happens to a deity with no worshippers?"

Dario straightened. "I see the other side of that coin. What happens when a deity does not leave when their job is over? Are they feted, or reviled?"

"And there's another angle." Zhulija ran her fingers over a coloured thread in the cloth. "If the seasons are their work, it's reasonable to assume their 'off' time is for relaxation, or a holiday. What happens to a deity when they've no choice but to work full time?"

"Exactly!" Lyssica pointed a finger at her sister. "The Cailleach probably doesn't want to work non-stop. Who would?"

A smile spread across Dario's face. "And there we have the Bodach's weak spot. His gift of eternal winter won't be received with the joy he believes. His Cailleach will, more than likely, be angry with him, and there's little happiness, or satisfaction, in a relationship where your woman eyes you with fury." He blew Zhulija a kiss.

She poked her tongue out at him. "I'll sort you out later."

His smile broadened. "I can't wait, my darling." She blushed, but her eyes narrowed and she wagged a finger. He blew another kiss.

A brush of fur, a prick of claws. *'See! That how romance done. More than hot skin and driving, wet ding-dong. Although, that rrowwrr.'* A tide of raw red prickled up Emryn's neck and surged across his face. "Be quiet!" He kept his voice to a mutter, but everyone stared.

"What?" Came from Lyssica.

Emryn cleared his throat. "Nothing. Just responding to Kynth-cat's internal musings." Dario's grin was knowing. Emryn bared a fang, something common to both his forms. "Getting back to the matter at hand—"

"Is it?" Dario elbowed him, grinning like a hyena. "At hand? Don't let us interrupt your private time."

Certain he was about to burst into flame from the heat in his cheeks, Emryn groaned and face palmed.

Lyssica looked to be fighting her own grin as she gave a laughing Zhulija a good-natured shove. "If I might interrupt—"

"I'm certain Emryn would love you to do so." Dario's voice was a suggestive purr.

"Oh!" A wide-eyed Lyssica was also overcome by a blush. "You're really very good at this, Dario."

Dario winked. "Practice. You just continue practicing with Emryn and you're well on your way to nirvana."

Both Zhulija's hands flattened on the table top. "I think that's enough, Dario. If you're trying to help Lyss see there's a much more enjoyable side to sex, I believe she's already discovering that."

"Yes." Lyssica nodded, cheeks still pink. "To be able to talk so openly about ..."

Dropping his hand from his face, Emryn reached to grasp her fingers again. "The good side and the bad? Yeah, it's cathartic, healing and healthy to speak and share and even joke; the sort of thing that abounds in loving relationships and amongst good friends." He twisted to look at Dario and Zhulija. "Although I've interacted with Dario in the past, I know we've only come to know each other properly since I arrived for the Tri-moon program, six and a half weeks ago. In that time, I've recognised you as friends

I'd be happy to commit to for life and, I hope you might see me in the same light – or manage to, before I must return home."

"Oh, Emryn, that's so lovely." Zhulija sighed. "I'm pleased to be your friend for life."

Dario offered his right arm and Emryn raised his in answer. As they clasped arms, Dario looked at him squarely. "You know it. Eternal friendship between us. Wherever we are."

This time, Zhulija pointed at Emryn. "And you may have to leave, but you'd better come back – or else."

Emryn laughed. "Or else?"

She wagged her finger at him. "I can do unpleasant things with a storm of loose objects – any loose objects." She raised her eyebrows. "Consider yourself warned."

And even though she'd added a light hearted touch, Emryn didn't mistake her intent. He looked to Lyssica; she winked at him.

CHAPTER THIRTEEN

LYSSICA

Firmly astride Kynthcat's back, fingers wrapped in the strands of his mane as she peered between his gnarled horns, Lyssica recognised the final bend in the road to Papillion. Beneath her, muscles bunched as his loping gait slowed and he headed for a copse of witherbeech saplings at the side of the road. Circling to the rear, where saplings screened them from the road, Kynthcat crouched, allowing Lyssica to slide to the ground. As she steadied herself, his big head swung around and a large rasping tongue slurped wetly across her face.

"Emryn!" She shoved him. "Urrk, I'm drowning. Blargh." He chuffed, ribs shaking as she scrubbed her face against his shoulder. "Stand still, you fluffy buffoon." Grinning, she unlatched the strap holding their pack, pulled the satchel away and watched, spell-bound, as a shimmering swirl of magical light enveloped Kynthcat. When the magic shimmer faded, Fae-male Emryn stood laughing at her. Naked Emryn. He looked so delicious she couldn't stop some very lustful thoughts from swamping her mind.

He winked. "I thought you liked my kisses."

Her eyes ran over him again and she licked her lips. "So, I do, just wasn't expecting Kynthcat's huge tongue bath." She thrust the bag towards him. "Here. Find some clothes and put them on before I get any ideas. We need to go home and work." Accepting the satchel, he dropped it to the ground, then reached for her.

"Ideas? I like the sound of that. How about some loving first? Having you snuggled on my back was very invigorating." He grinned as he folded his arms around her. "If you know what I mean."

She raised her face, her mouth as eager as his, their connection equally as wonderful as it'd been every time since their first night two weeks prior. His taste, his scent, the way he held her. It simply felt right, like tab A and slot B had found their perfect connection. Her fingers threaded into the hair at the nape of his neck, sifting through the strands to stroke the skin beneath.

He shuddered, rocking against her; his erection large and thick between them. Lyssica gasped and rubbed the peaks of her aching breasts across his bare chest.

"Time sands, you're a sweet delight, Lyss."

She kissed him again, a full flowering of her mouth over his, before drawing back for breath. "The idea of being in the open for our loving is strangely compelling, but I'd like to choose a time when we're not in a hurry. Also, it's cold and damp."

He sighed. "Much as I hate it, you're right." Bestowing another lingering kiss before he released her, Emryn bent to their pack. Pulling his trousers free, he sat and dragged them on. Lyssica licked her lips as a loose tunic concealed most of his gorgeous chest, the laces left untied. Next were socks and finally a pair of baggy-topped, calf boots. Standing, he shouldered the now closed bag and held out his hand. "Ready?"

Smiling, she grabbed hold and they returned to the road. Emryn halted them, his fingers tipping her chin up so they could look into each other's eyes. "Lyss, I've been thinking about this." His throat worked, then words rushed out of him. "I love being with you and I'll proudly acknowledge our relationship. Your choice, but I don't want you to feel uncomfortable or to have anyone think we're sneaking around. However, if you prefer to keep our closeness a secret ..."

Her smile was tender as she stood on tip toes and brushed her mouth over his. "I'm at the point where I don't care what anybody else thinks. I won't hide our connection – I've no wish to."

Emryn's kiss was firmer. "Excellent." He kissed her again, mouth lingering. "Thoughts of you consume my days, but I'm not going to embarrass you, or your family, by behaving in an unprofessional manner during work sessions."

Lyssica rested her head against the side of his neck, one hand smoothing the chest of his tunic. "I can't keep you out of my mind either." She sighed dreamily. "At least we're spending all our nights at Garadenya."

He nodded. "Yes, we can be ourselves with Zhu and Dario." He drew her hand up to his mouth, kissed the palm, then relinquished it. Bowing, he made a sweeping gesture. "Lead on my delightful Heir-Lady Aphiski."

~

"We're back, Papan." Lyssica joined her father in his inner sanctum. "Safe and sound."

He grunted, looking her over. "Better late than never, I suppose." The duke's gaze shifted to her partner. "Greetings Emryn."

"Morning." The rumble of Emryn's voice vibrated through the connection where his chest met her back. She wanted to rub herself against him; instead she shrugged.

"Things don't always go according to plan Papan."

Emryn turned a hand palm up. "Dario and I were making plans this morning for future lessons. Time got away from us. Our apologies, Yanvian."

Her father grunted, massaging his temple. "Probably not important today anyway. We need a break from the guests, so I gave them the day off. Tomorrow, two will go to the barn and two to the stables for the morning, then swap for the afternoon. They'll be learning animal husbandry and how it relates to the estate's occupants. That gives you almost two days off." He glanced between them. "So, no need to rush back to Papillion tomorrow, if you'd rather stay with Zhu and Dario and rest."

Lyssica blinked in surprise. "Oh. Thank you, Papan. A day of relaxation will be wonderful."

"Yes, well, it's been a long six weeks and you've been looking tired lately." He shuffled papers on his desk. "I know you've taken on a heavy schedule and it hasn't been easy." He paused, gaze sweeping both of them. "Also, the more I've come to know Perris Momphiday, the happier I am Emryn is guarding you."

Lyssica tensed. Beside her Emryn's tautness radiated through their shoulder connection. "What do you mean, Papan? He's said or done something to um, upset you?"

Duke Yanvian methodically stacked his papers inside a folder. "I'm watching all our guests closely. I've reports to provide on this program and I like to be thorough – I require your opinions, too."

A smile lit Lyssica's face. "I'm pleased to contribute. But what did you mean, about Perris?"

Her father's eyes narrowed. "I'll get to him. First, the others." He massaged his chin. "Kerrigold is strong and determined – her heart's not really in this type of learning, but she's giving it her all."

Lyssica nodded. "I agree with that. Plus she confessed to me she has an artistic bent and would really love to talk with Zhu before she goes home."

"Ah." Yanvian pursed his lips. "We can arrange that." He nodded. "Melkaz is keen and interested. He's got a brain and he'll be an excellent partner for whoever he ends up with in the future."

"Yes." Lyssica tilted her head. "Plus, he's insightful and always a gentleman."

"Good. Moving on to Venaday." The duke's mouth turned down. "Although he acts doltish, he's smarter than one would think. He's giving lip service to the lessons but is persisting with his Private Investigation goal. I've suggested he seek an apprenticeship in that field."

Lyssica frowned, clasping her hands in front of her. "Venaday gives lip service to anything he's not absolutely invested in, but, if he is interested, he'll give all of his attention. I sometimes think the doltish act is a cover up."

Her father nodded. "You could be right. I hadn't thought of that." He frowned. "So, then there's Perris. On the surface, he's friendly, affable, always smiling – talks well and listens attentively. But ..."

"But?"

Duke Yanvian's eyes moved from Emryn to Lyssica. "Don't ever turn your back on him. Don't rely on him, don't trust him and don't ever make the mistake of thinking he's your friend."

Lyssica could only stare at her father. She bit her tongue to refrain from revealing how correct he was.

Emryn's soft voice filled her silence. "That's a very definitive assessment."

Yanvian's mouth twisted. "Like I said, I've been observing. So has Entanglit, at my request. The actions and interactions of Perris Momphiday are concerning. His smiles fade quickly when no-one is looking. They never reach his eyes. He sneaks around and listens to conversations before he enters a room. He lies. He puts people down, denigrates them under the guise of camaraderie and jokes. In my opinion he's an unpleasant sort."

Lyssica swallowed, decided to be truthful. "I confess he makes my skin crawl."

A low growl vibrated from Emryn. "I have ensured Lyssica is never alone with anyone but Kerrigold. Be certain I'll take extra care with him."

"Good. I'm glad we're in agreement." Stepping away from his desk, Duke Yanvian approached. "Lunch was put back to await your arrival; let's go and eat before it becomes dinner."

Lyssica's eyes widened. "Oh, Papan, you didn't have to wait for us." To her surprise, her father linked one arm with hers and the other with Emryn's.

"We chose to. Your mother and I decided we'd rather eat with family instead of strangers, even if they are guests."

Used to her father's gruff solemnity, Lyssica couldn't believe her ears. *'Who are you and what have you done with Papan?'*

Two weeks later, Lyssica huffed out a frosty breath and eyed the snow drifts gloomily. Beneath her, Kynthcat's large paws forged a path through the forest's frozen undergrowth. The snow continued to fall with an increasing regularity of blizzards, even though Auguary's last winter moon was waning. In another week it'd be dark moon night – the official end of winter and the beginning of spring. The vernal Spring Equinox was six days later. *Ostara Day in two weeks and I've made no progress!* She swiped at the tiny ice crystals on the tips of her lashes.

Impatience was a live coal burning her gut. She'd given sodding Perris Momphiday plenty of opportunity to approach and ask to speak with her privately, but he'd remained distant. She didn't understand. He watched her all the time when she and Emryn were at Papillion. Early in the program he'd asked for meetings several times, unhappy when she'd brushed him off, so what was he playing at now?

It wasn't as if she could invite Perris to ask her for a private meeting – not without making him suspicious as to her motives. And then there was the devil-rabbit – was it waiting for an invitation to participate in skulduggery? No. On a daily basis, bodies of hibernating animals were found ripped from their dens and left lying broken and bloody in the snow. She'd been able to heal many of them with slow but steady bursts of power; the survivors conveyed images of night attacks by Vulpiawolves guided by a large, nasty smelling rabbit.

Kynthcat slowed at the sight of more Vulpia attack-webs. From a bag at her hip, Lyssica drew out some stones and lobbed them at web after web until all of them were tatters drifting on the wind. The ground became littered with acidic web scraps; luckily they'd disintegrate over the next several hours. Carefully navigating a way between the pieces, Kynthcat padded on, aiming for Ostara's circle, where Lyssica dismounted.

As she began her paean of song and dance in praise of Ostara, animals gathered. Squirrels, rabbits, duskits and possums rubbed shoulders with predatorial foxes, raccoons, badgers and even some skunweasels; Ostara blessed all of them equally. Emryn professed himself fascinated by the tiny duskits with their huge eyes, enormous ears and super fluffy tails on small bodies. There were none near his packlands and, to his mind, they looked to be a possum-fox hybrid. Throughout the ritual, Lyssica glimpsed him patrolling the borders of the circle; the animals now so used to his presence, Kynthcat was mostly ignored as he wove between them.

Sitting as she ended her final dance, Lyssica spread her arms in welcome. "Come little ones." She was immediately besieged by animals wanting to receive a goddess blessing. She kept the flow of power a continuous low wave, bathing all in affection, light and warmth. Her access to the power had slowed to a trickle, with the strange blockage and her inability to contact Ostara, but hadn't totally dried up, much to her relief.

Lyssica patted, cuddled, blessed and cooed while the afternoon waned, then allowed the power flow to die away. "I'm sorry, it's time for me to go. I'll be back tomorrow though." She was surprised to notice none of the animals had dispersed as they usually did. "You can go home now." Some sat down, others whined, but they continued to watch her, none of them departing. She hesitated, then looked up as Kynthcat appeared, making his way between the creatures. They moved for him, then closed in again. He looked at her, brows knitting; then chuffed, the sound low and questioning.

"I don't know why they're still here – do they want to see us off?" The fur of his shoulders rippled in a feline shrug before he lowered enough for her to swing astride. Straightening, he walked slowly through the crowd of animals. Lyssica turned to wave and froze. "Oh my Goddess! They're following us ..."

And they continued to follow all the way back to Garadenya, refusing to leave her vicinity.

Lyssica glanced over her shoulder, stunned by the horde of animals hurrying in their wake. More than previous days, the most since the exodus of animals from the forest had begun. Species which were normally enemies ran side by side, sometimes even helping each other. A baggage train of frightened, bewildered, hungry creatures, ill-equipped to survive the heavy winter and the persecution of the devil-rabbit with a pack of vicious Vulpiawolves.

Now, none of the animals who came to Ostara's circle for Lyssica's rituals left afterwards and, every day a new group came to participate, never leaving her side when she finished. After the first time, animals even waited by the side of the road to follow Lyssica and Emryn to the Papillion Estate in the morning, as well as to Garadenya in the late afternoon. Both estates had impromptu animal hostelries set up, with Duchesse Azura and Treymeron supervising the animals' welfare at Papillion, while Zhulija and Dario oversaw those who'd arrived at Garadenya. Lyssica marvelled at how many creatures the forest was home to.

Even more disquieting was the lack of actual confrontation with the devil-rabbit, particularly after the first terrible meeting through Roland Arrelgyre's body. There were no day sightings of Vulpiawolves either. It was as if they deliberately conducted their heinous violence, set their traps and poisoned the plant life in the dark hours of the night when Lyssica and Emryn were *not* in the forest. But during the day, it was a constant battle to undo as much harm as possible to the flora and fauna under siege.

Looking ahead, Lyssica sighed with relief as the Papillion gates appeared. A shout rose as they were sighted and one gate was opened for them. The gate guards stared past them, wide eyed at the number of animals in their retinue. Without prompting, Kynthcat headed directly for the stables at the back of the manor. That building, plus the barns, had been re-purposed to house the refugee wildlife.

It was no surprise to find Maman and Treymeron moving around the structures, directing volunteers from all over the estate in the care the animals required.

From the door of the stables, Treymeron waved. "Lyss! I need a word."

She waved acknowledgement and nudged Kynthcat. He halted, letting her slide from his back; she rubbed his shoulders affectionately as she went. He turned his head, lowering it to nuzzle her cheek, then made his way past Treymeron, into the stable.

Treymeron's dark black and violet eyes catalogued her. "Good to see you're okay, sis." He shook his head. "I can't believe all these animals – they just keep coming." Smiling widely, he provided a rundown on how everyone was coping, regardless of whether they were Fae-folk or forest dweller. "Even when you're not here, they accept and trust us."

"They scent Lyss on you, that's why." A dressed, two-legged Emryn reached them. "Thanks for staying with her while I changed."

Lyssica smiled. "You're loving this, aren't you Trey?"

One of his hands did a side-to-side juggle. "Part of it. I love the ability to interact with them like this, but I'm angry at the reason for it. The winters here have never been so severe." He glanced around, sighed. "It's unnatural for them to be cooped up, but we're doing the best we can and they seem to understand."

A tiny duskit, it's variegated purple fur brilliant against the snow-covered ground, squeaked as it drew up at their feet, huge ears flickering and large eyes liquid. A tiny paw tugged at the hem of Treymeron's trouser leg. "Aw." Bending, he scooped the small creature up and snuggled it into his neck. "It's okay, little one. I know you miss your maman. I'll take you upstairs to join the others in a moment."

Reaching out, Lyssica stroked the duskit baby with one finger. "The others?"

"Yeah, Papan has a basket with a few duskit orphans in his office. He said it was the warmest place for them, but I don't know." One eyebrow wigged up and down. "I popped in late yesterday and he had them on his lap."

Lyssica goggled. "Papan? Are we talking about the same Fae-male who sired us?"

"Yeah." He grinned as Emryn broke into a coughing fit. "Not what I expected."

"I know, right?" Lyssica shook her head. "A couple of weeks ago he told me he'd prefer to spend time with family, instead of guests. I thought there was something wrong with him. Now, he's snuggling orphan duskits? Wow."

Her brother nodded. "I've noticed changes too. Perhaps he's mellowing? Who knows, but that's not what I wanted to talk about."

"What's up, Trey?"

He glanced around, sidled closer. "That Perris Momphiday ..." His lip curled. "I don't like him. He's a slimy bastard."

"Good instincts."

"Yeah, well, he's been trying to befriend me. He asks questions about you all the time. Wants to know your schedule. I dodge him as much as possible. Lately he's been saying there's something between you and him."

Disgust welled in Lyssica. "There's not."

"Didn't think so." He folded his arms." He says you knew him well a few years ago. That true?"

"Unfortunately, yes." Her voice barely carried above the rattling growl in Emryn's chest. "It's okay, Emryn." She swallowed. "Trey, I need your help."

"What is it, Lyss?"

She pressed her lips together, gathered her courage. "We knew each other during my party years. He – he took advantage of me and my foolishness." She couldn't look at her younger brother, just couldn't.

Fingers under her chin raised her face to meet Trey's concerned gaze. "He harmed you?"

"Yes, but I'm okay and I won't let him make a victim of me. I won't *be* a victim, ever again."

Trey narrowed his eyes. "Hell. I'll kill that piece of—"

A deep snarl from Emryn. "Get in line."

Trey's brows skyrocketed. "Get in line? What's that supposed to mean?"

Fingers over her lips, Lyssica blinked at her little brother. Since when had he faced-off against others like this?

Emryn's smiled mirthlessly. "It means Dario and I are way ahead of you."

Lyssica touched Trey's forearm, brought his gaze back to her. "That's where I'd like your help. Dario is a Queen's agent but not on private land, unless he has a warrant, which he doesn't."

Trey cocked his head. "So you need Momphiday on crown land. The forest?"

She nodded. "Would you be willing to tell him I'll be at Ostara's Circle tomorrow afternoon? And Emryn will be leaving me to go hunting because I feel safe there?"

"So, he'll think you're alone?" Trey rubbed his chin. "Yeah, I'll do that." He cast a sly look at Emryn. "Hunting, eh? I just won't tell him he's the prey."

CHAPTER FOURTEEN

EMRYN

"The swine fell for it!" Grinning, Treymeron punched the air as they met him at the postern gate later that afternoon. "I told Momphiday your schedule's busy and I wasn't sure when you could meet him, Lyss. He pressed for details, sprinkling his questions while we cared for the animals in the barn." He snorted. "I dropped information about your daily visits to Ostara's Circle where it's so safe, Emryn often wanders off hunting. He asked me how to find the circle and after I explained about the path, he left me alone."

Emryn clapped Treymeron's shoulder. "Good work."

The younger Fae-male flexed his wings, firmed his stance, then focused on his sister. "I'd like to help, Lyss. What more can I do?" A purple furry head with large ears and night dark eyes, popped out of the neck of his voluminous cloak and chittered.

Lyssica blinked. "Oh." Smiling, she stretched a cautious hand to stroke the tiny duskit. "Look at you." Her voice was a low croon. "So cute and innocent." She flicked her brother a look. "I thought you were taking this one to add to Papan's orphan group?"

Slight colour flushed Treymeron's cheeks. "Yeah, well, I did, but she wouldn't stay there. I tried a couple of times, but every time I left, she followed me." He shrugged. "I caved in. It was easier to keep her with me while I was working than to constantly run up to Papan's office. I fashioned a small sling against my chest and she seems warm and comfortable."

Emryn tickled the baby duskit under her chin, watching her in fascination. Eyes closed, she lapped up the combined attention of both he and Lyssica. "I'd never seen duskits until I came here. There's none in the hills and valleys of the Pack territories."

Treymeron pursed his mouth. "Maybe that's because the climate is too warm?"

Withdrawing his hand to adjust a strap on his pack, Emryn nodded. "As good a reason as any, I suppose." His gaze was drawn to Lyssica as she cooed at the baby duskit; she was so gorgeous, gentle and kind. He hated to break the moment but … "Time to go, Lyss. There's more snow coming."

She studied the sky. "No argument from me." Turning to Treymeron, she pursed her lips. "I don't know what other chores to give you, Trey. You're already doing a lot by helping the animals – maybe keep an eye on Perris for me?"

"Yeah." He nodded. "I'll certainly do that." Leaning to kiss her cheek, he tried a hug but it proved awkward with the duskit snuggled in between. "You be careful now." Treymeron pointed at Emryn. "And you, too, Mr Kynthcat – you're the biggest bonus to come out of this swap program."

Smiling widely, warmth pushing up inside him like a furnace, Emryn exchanged a warrior's arm clasp with Treymeron. "Thank you. I will be sad to return home when this is over."

"You're welcome here any time." Tucking the duskit into her sling and wrapping his cloak firmly about himself, Treymeron slipped into the bushes.

Outside the gate, Emryn escorted Lyssica across the road to the bushy undergrowth at the edge of the forest where he dropped his pack and began stripping. Lyssica grabbed the bag and undid the clasps, holding it open for Emryn's clothes. He tossed them in, then straightened, gratified to see her eyes moved boldly over his nakedness.

She licked her lips, then offered an uncertain smile. "It will be awful to see you go, but we knew our relationship was going to be short term."

He kissed her, even as his eyes reflected pain. "Never thought I'd say this, but I hate the idea of leaving – you're a delight I hadn't expected. How is it we mesh so well when we're from such different worlds?"

Her lips trembled. "I hadn't thought to ever meet someone as wonderful as you, but yes, our personal obligations have us at a disadvantage."

His Adam's apple bobbed. "We need to think how we might get around your commitments here, both to the estate as Heir-Lady and as Ostara's Handmaiden; or my tether and commitments to the pack." He feared there *wasn't* a way and his heart weighed heavy inside him.

Kynthcat hissed, clawing at him sharply. *'No leave our mate. We steal her.'* Emryn flinched, but shook his head, unable to take his eyes from Lyssica.

She closed the pack, fiddled with a clasp. "You've mentioned that tether before. What do you mean? What is it?"

"Fair question." Emryn nodded. "It's part of shape-changer magic. A psychic link to our Alpha and, through him, a tenuous connection to other pack mates. The Alpha has one with every member of the pack. It's a permanent bond ensuring personal and emotional safety; no-one is ever alone, lost, or feels like they don't belong. It also acts like a ... leash, I guess, for want of a better word. Wherever we are, the link stretches, but after a time we have to go home to re-charge because we're Pack. We're one, we're connected." He scratched his head. "I'm not sure I'm explaining it very well; it's never been needed before."

Lyssica didn't meet his eyes. "I think I understand." She hesitated. "Is it ever broken?"

Emryn's nose wrinkled. "Sometimes, but only for extreme

reasons and any loners eventually go mad. For some reason, shape-changers *need* that psychic link of belonging somewhere."

Kynthcat snarled inside him. *'NOT leave our mate!'*

'You keep saying 'mate', but you can't possibly be right.' Emryn sought his change and dropped to all fours, becoming Kynthcat. *'You know we only mate with other shape-changers.'*

But, now that he'd morphed, Kynthcat was in charge and he roared their anger and denial to the sky, coughed, then roared again. His heart throbbed with anguish, but they were helpless against the power of the Pack tether.

Lyssica thwacked their ribs with the satchel, her voice a hiss. "That's certainly making a statement, but was it a good idea to announce our presence so loudly? Get down and give me a chance to mount up, you big oaf." Recalled to their senses, the extra air gathered for another roar left his lungs in a rush and he dropped to lie prone on the ground. Lyssica slung the divided bag across his shoulders then slid into position behind it. Once she'd settled, Kynthcat rose, padding deeper into the forest, following the ribbon of track barely visible under a thin coat of snow.

When they reached Ostara's circle, Kynthcat waited for Lyssica to slide off, before stalking back into the brush at the circle's edge. Behind him, Lyssica burst into song, her voice soaring as she began her daily ritual.

Patrolling the boundaries as had become his habit, Kynthcat threaded between trees and around bushes. At the far side of the circle, a faint but nasty scent assailed his nostrils and saturated his tongue – that of black snow and putrid mud. He propped, spitting in an effort to vent the cloying nastiness. There was no mistaking it, the devil-rabbit had been here earlier. Uneasily, he cast around some more, also picking up the wet fur aroma of Vulpiawolves; a lot of them.

Casting a glance back towards the circle, he glimpsed Lyssica dancing around each of Ostara's blessed rock tors, crooning to the heavens, arms outstretched. Still safe. He nodded, confident enough in her safety to see if he could discover which way the devil-rabbit had gone. Following the smell, sometimes nosing the ground, other times tasting the air with his tongue, he realised it was strengthening. But he was now well out of sight of Lyssica, had gone further than he intended and that unsettled him. Time to return, but just as he turned back, the flutter of wings came from above.

"Psst! Emryn, Kynthcat!"

Glancing up, he was surprised to find Treymeron hovering, his sooty wings with their cream, violet, lavender and cobalt blue markings spread wide.

"Momphiday didn't stick to the script, he followed you *today*. Get to Lyss, the swine's nearly to the circle."

'Damn!' He morphed quickly from Kynthcat to Fae-male form. "Dario was meant to be here to apprehend the cretin. Can you fly to Garadenya while we hold the fort here?" He barely heard Treymeron's hasty agreement before again becoming Kynthcat and spinning to race for Ostara's rocks. His heart beat out her name with every stride. *'Lyssica! Lyssica! Lyssica!'*

No time to freak out, this was battle. Slowing, he forced himself to slink closer, stopping behind a large bush to survey the scene. Perris Momphiday had halted a few steps inside the circle, just beyond where the path truncated, watching Lyssica who swayed as she serenaded Ostara, arms reaching to the sky. Near her, animals had gathered, waiting for her attention. Slowly, Lyssica lowered her arms and dropped to her knees, facing the nearest creatures.

Her words tripped out, softly lilting. "I'm ready, sweet ones, come to me."

Perris grinned. "Oh, I have, dear Lyssica, I have."

Stiffening, Lyssica turned her head, pinning a narrow-eyed stare on the interloper. "You're not welcome here, Perris. This is goddess business. At least have the decency to wait until it's completed."

"Pfft!" Perris waved a dismissive hand. "No need to pretend. We both know that's a lot of twaddle you invented."

She shook her head. "Your opinion is irrelevant. What do you want?"

Perris' slow smile was all teeth. "You. I want you. Unless you agree to consort with me, I'll tell your father, mother, family—" He spread his arms. "Demonhells, why stop with them? I'll tell the world that you're an impure slut."

Her stare was icy. "You really are contemptible. I feel sorry for your parents. You don't need me. You've already taken what you wanted."

He shrugged. "I've no problem having it again. Who wouldn't want a cushy position in life with a beautiful Fae-female at his beck and call? Then you'll inherit that magnificent estate and I'll be in position to take it over."

She tilted her head. "My Papan may live for many more years, you realise?"

His lips twisted in a sneer. "Accidents happen."

"I'll stop you."

"Not if you know what's good for you."

Inspired by Lyssica's calm command, Kynthcat dug his claws into the earth, fighting to emulate her serenity, when all his savagery urged him to pounce, to rip and tear, to rend this poor excuse for a Fae-male into bloody bits. Struggling to mute the snarls rattling his chest, Kynthcat tensed with hatred. *'Want kill male.'*

This Fae-male was a low-life bastard who deserved to pay for hurting Lyssica – in the past and for the hurts he planned to commit. But Kynthcat held his naturally bloodthirsty nature in, watched and waited, eyes savage with promise. The ball was in Lyssica's court.

Animals clustered around her. Glancing over them, she stroked the fur of as many as she could reach, then clapped her hands softly. "Go and hide little ones. Be safe and we'll commune later." They obeyed, scampering away. Perris Momphiday cleared his throat loudly.

"I don't like being ignored by my future consort."

"I know what's good for me; it isn't you." Lyssica stood, dusting herself off, meeting her tormentor's gaze squarely. "I'm declining your less than generous offer, Perris."

His eyes widened. "What do you mean you decline? You can't! Didn't you hear me say I'd tell everyone of your shame?"

She laughed scornfully. "*Your* shame, not mine. Back then, I was a victim, drugged and helpless. I'm not one now. I don't care who you tell – I'm proud of who I am. I doubt you can say the same about yourself." Deliberately, she looked him up and down. "It's obvious you're nothing but a stinking sleazebag."

His expression turned ugly. "Why you!" He leapt towards her. Still crouched, Kynthcat sprang into the circle, but halted as Lyssica twisted into a sideways jump, extending her leg and angling her foot to create a sharp edge. Perris impaled himself, his forward motion ramming her bladed foot deep into his stomach. Her momentum, fuelled with the anger of years, drove him backwards; the air whooshing from him. He flew through the ether before landing heavily on the frozen ground where he flailed feebly, gasping for air. Lyssica landed lightly, followed through on her action and kept moving until she stood poised with her heel above his throat.

"I know what you are and you don't frighten me, Perris. Give me one good reason not to crush your windpipe."

Stunned but proud, Kynthcat didn't intervene. Lyssica had this. All they had to do now was wait for Dario to arrive and this thug would be dealt with. He heard a whisper of sound behind them and twisted, cursing his preoccupation. And went down under a storm of Vulpiawolves, no match for their combined fangs, claws and webs.

CHAPTER FIFTEEN

LYSSICA

*P*ositioned threateningly over Perris, Lyssica twisted her head towards the snarls and growls; horror swamped her as a tangle of fighting animals rolled out into the open clearing. The green and grey Vulpiawolves were easily recognised.

"No!" She caught glimpses of Kynthcat's coppery hide, the curl of a horn, a flash of his deep brown mane, but over, above and around him was a seething, ferocious sea of spiky green-grey fur, dark grey skin, and barbed tails. The snarling, biting, flailing mass writhed across the ground – there were so many. Anguish filled her, came out in the scream of her voice. "Emryn!"

Beneath her, the desperate hands of Perris scrabbled at her mid-air foot and pushed. Losing her balance, she toppled sideways, but recovered even as she landed, crouching on the balls of her feet, one knee resting on the ground, hands on either side of her.

Turning her head, she expected to see Perris advancing on her, but he hadn't moved.

Lyssica sucked in a breath. Over him stood the devil-rabbit, clawed paws digging into Perris's neck, lips peeled back over sharp fangs. Ignoring Perris' gurgles, the creature's gimlet eyes swivelled up to Lyssica; it grinned, shaking its head, tossing the long, floppy ears to-and-fro.

Struggling with the black snow and putridly muddy aroma of the creature, Lyssica choked. Then the filthy miasma of its linked death magic wafted on the breeze and she instinctively jerked on her Ostara powers, covering herself in a cloak of Ostara's fertile life force as she'd done the last time they'd met. Her breathing eased instantly.

"We meet again, Chosen of Ostara." The devil-rabbit grinned, its head tilted, prominent snout wiggling. "I scent the perfidy of this male on the ground. He hunted you. We can't have that. You're *our* prey." Without taking its eyes off her, the devil-rabbit dug its claws deep into Perris's throat and ripped sideways. Blood gushed and Perris's whimpering died; he sagged like a wet airbag.

Adjusting to full height, the devil-rabbit licked a bloody claw, paused, then licked the rest of Perris's blood away and smiled. "No distraction now, is there, Chosen of Ostara?"

Deliberately, Lyssica flung her life-force cloak at the devil-rabbit, pushing the power of Ostara's fertile life at the abomination. It squealed as the power cloak, visible only to Lyssica, covered it completely. She kept on force feeding power into the cloak, while the creature shrilled and struggled, muzzle drawn back in a rictus of agony. Sinking to the ground under her onslaught, it began to draw in upon itself, shrinking rapidly.

Lyssica gulped, raising her hands to cover her ears, but she kept the pressure of power up as the devil-rabbit shrank until finally, the last handful of it poofed away in a noxious cloud of black smoke. All that remained was the taint of its vile odour.

Cutting the flow of power meant her life-force cloak vanished as well. She'd reform it later; Emryn needed help now and she frantically hoped she wasn't too late.

Pain flowering inside her at the thought, she shot to her feet, then stopped as the ether trembled where she'd destroyed the devil-rabbit. Staring transfixed at the air shimmering like a minia-ture heat wave, she clenched her fists as a new figure took shape. Dismay filled her.

Hovering in the air was the solid, thickly muscled figure of a much older male. He wore ragged clothing, chewed on a long straw of dried grass, and an ancient, broad brimmed hat perched low on his head, like a dark mushroom cap. Black, watchful eyes assessed her from under the hat's curled brim. "I felt the yank as my rabbit-golem was destroyed. That makes me unhappy, Chosen of Ostara." Long claws, deadly as scimitars, flashed out from the tips of his fingers, gleaming in the wintry light.

Swallowing, Lyssica danced backward, but the old male covered the distance she'd achieved in one powerful leap, forcing her to continue retreating. She only stopped when her spine thumped into one of Ostara's tall rocks, her intent to dart sideways foiled at the sensation of cold, hard claws at her throat. The long, dagger-sharp tips pricked her skin, while his mouth stretched into a grotesque rictus of pleasure.

"What fun you've been, little upstart Fae."

Lyssica stared defiantly down her nose. "Who *are* you?"

He grinned. "Why, I'm the Bodach, of course."

She glared at him. "The cause of this entire mess. I hope you realise never-ending winter is a curse not a gift."

He stared at her, eyebrows shooting up until they disappeared under his hat brim. "How do you know my plan?" He scowled. "Never mind, what's your meaning?"

Lyssica snorted her disgust. "You'll be making your Cailleach work. All the time. Non-stop. Do you think she'll thank you for that?" Over the terrible old creature's shoulder, she saw Kynthcat drag himself from beneath a furry mass, his gaze fixated on her, then he stumbled and went down under a fresh pile of Vulpia-wolves. Drops of red sprinkled the snow.

"No!" She couldn't hold back her cry of horror and the blood drained from her face, leaving her light-headed. She swayed, feeling the dig of the Bodach's claws, then Kynthcat howled, his ringing call of defiance an indication he yet lived. She straightened, fisted her hands as he reappeared, a swirl of brown mane and copper fur, horns swiping viciously, even as the Vulpiawolf pack hemmed him in, snapping and lunging. Several attacked from behind, their weight combining to ride him to the ground. The pack swarmed again and this time when the melee cleared, Kynthcat's form was limp, great horned head lolling as they dragged him to the nearest tree and bound him to the trunk with their icy web.

Lyssica's heart sank. Emryn and Kynthcat were trapped and she was helpless at the mercy of the Bodach.

Perhaps she'd lost, but she still had words for weapons. "What a poor excuse for a consort you are. If the Cailleach only knew what you've been doing, she'd be so disappointed."

Mouth twisted with displeasure, the Bodach crooked a finger. A Vulpiawolf responded, closing in to slap some web across her mouth, cheeks and chin. It hardened, stinging icily, but at least it didn't hurt as much as the attack-web they produced. He smirked. "That's shut you up."

Panting and furious, Lyssica fought despair over a failure more than personal. She hadn't lived up to Ostara's trust, she'd failed Emryn and let her family, and everyone relying on her, down. Worse, her defeat left the world open to the Bodach's evil actions. Pictures of the Fae-Demesnes locked in a bitter eternal winter flashed through her mind. Scene after scene of hardship, persecution and despair – for the Fae-folk, for all the animals and plants. Winter forever meant no new plant life and any young animals birthed would either die of cold or be slaughtered indiscriminately by the Vulpiawolves for food and sport. Blood would stain the snow, flowing in rivers like the lashings of redberry syrup Treymeron loved on his ice cream.

Lump in her throat, Lyssica bit her lip to stop tears as she stared across the clearing towards Emryn; Kynthcat was now alert and thrashing at his icy Vulpia-web bindings. An anguished roar escaped him as their eyes locked and suddenly she was flooded with tangled feelings, a knotty mass that rocked her empathic senses with ferocious intensity. Within the mass, fear and despair battled for supremacy. He was afraid for *her*, terrified that she would die and he be unable to save her. Oh, how she loved him for that.

She faltered. She loved him? Yes! Of course she did. She'd never have committed so much of herself to him if ...

A sharp slap to both cheeks snapped her head askew and only the hard rock at her back kept her upright.

"None of that." Still gleeful, the Bodach shook his head. His claws still hovered at her neck but had retreated a little. "I'll not allow it. Lots of creatures try disassociation of the mind by hiding inside themselves – I thought you were braver than that, Chosen of Ostara."

She was. Oh yes, she was. She'd conceded defeat too soon, shouldn't have given up in the slightest. Thrusting her face over his dagger sharp claws, she snagged the Vulpia-web covering her mouth and yanked.

Snap!

Crisp shards of icy web splintered free, to fall in frozen spicules and spray across the snowy ground. Snatching a breath and her courage, Lyssica started to sing, words of sunlight, of growth, of spring welling up inside her, pouring out of her mouth. Her triumph swelled as the Bodach hissed and trembled in fury, as Kynthcat lifted his head in hope, as—

The Bodach snarled, thrust his paw between her open jaws, snagged claws into her tongue and yanked.

His longest dagger claw flashed.

There was a brief pain; she tasted blood ...

And time slowed as her tongue cartwheeled through the air in endless lazy spirals. With a loud splat, it hit the snow, bouncing and rolling before it came to rest – an almost obscene blob of pink flesh, bloody, forlorn and abandoned.

Lyssica's vision began to blacken at the edges, her legs trembled, then gave way and she slid down the stone to collapse on the ground. She was barely aware of Kynthcat's roars of rage and distress and the Bodach's howls of laughter. Prodding her with his foot, he rolled her to her back, still laughing as he stared down into her dazed eyes. "Tell me off now, Chosen of Ostara." His words mocked. "How about you sing for me." He tipped his head sideways. "What? You can't? Ostara must be so disappointed in you."

'Ostara, my Goddess.' Lyssica pushed back the pain, the dizziness in her mind to access their internal meeting place, not surprised to find it still surrounded by fog. For days, she'd come here, calling and calling, using her power to batter at the fog, needing advice and assistance from Ostara and each time she'd had no success. Now, dizzy, bloody and despairing, she aimed and sent a thin mental dart, a cry of distress. She envisioned the tiny sharp point finding a way through when solid battering had gotten her nowhere. *'Ostara, I need your help!'*

The power of Ostara's mental response was a burst of sunlight, dispersing the fog in seconds, reading Lyssica's open and willing mind, reliving her memories of the events through the winter, of the Bodach's perfidious plan and her current hopeless situation.

The Bodach prodded her again. "I'd expected more from you, but there it is. A Handmaiden is no match for a Demigod."

She didn't respond to his taunts. Couldn't. Her body was filling with power like she'd never felt before. It swept to her extremities, enervating her senses, imbuing her with joy and a strength beyond her imaginings. The process made her body spasm as magic flooded her body.

The Consort of the Winter Queen grinned down at her spasming form. "Looks like I win."

"Not just yet, Bodach." Despite her state, Lyssica recognised Dario's voice. "Come, feel my fire." Lyssica managed to force her eyes open. Closing in on them was a two-legged figure wreathed in flames.

The Bodach whistled. "Oho, what have we here? The infamous Unseelie Beast challenges me. Ouch!"

A second fireball followed the first. "You talk too much."

The Bodach howled. "I'll put your flames out, see if I don't!" He began muttering, then lifted his face and arms to the sky and broke into a loud chant. "Ice, I call you, snow I command you, storms, I summon you. Let this blizzard destroy my foes and herald the beginning of eternal winter. In the name of The Cailleach, I—"

"Nngh!" Lunging forward, Lyssica wrapped a hand around the Bodach's ankle and opened the floodgates on her new power. It sizzled through her fingertips and into his body.

Screaming incoherently, he toppled to the ground. Lyssica held tight and wriggled until her other hand touched his other leg. Her instincts urged her to sing, but her mouth was an empty cavity except for the blood. A thought bloomed: *I still have my vocal cords; I can make noise.*

Certain it was a message from Ostara, Lyssica opened her mouth and let sound flow out, despite the pain. The wordless song was intertwined with the power of spring, of flowers and growth, of sunshine and light rain showers, of fertility and rebirth. She let it pour out of her in a continuous stream, a paean of joy and beauty. To her amazement, the well of force was ceaseless, no matter how much she poured into her voice and then, through her hands – it just kept coming.

Eventually, a hand touched her arm. "Lyssica, amazing as this is, you can stop now. He's unconscious, and so are the Vulpiawolves." Dario's voice was gentle.

Cutting the flow of energy, Lyssica simply dropped her head to the ground and lay there. But the new power was still a volcano bubbling inside, blooming and circling in a constant joyous effervescence of life and spirit. Surging to her feet, she hugged Dario exuberantly, then bolted across the circle toward where Kynthcat lay bloody amidst a ring of prostrate Vulpiawolves. He stirred as she reached him, eyes blinking open dazedly. She ran her hands over him, cooing wordlessly and the sparkling, healing current flowed from her to him like water. His Vulpia-web bindings melted away under the onslaught, wounds began to knit and bare seconds later he morphed, jerked to a sitting position and grasped her arms.

"Lyssica!" Emryn stared at her urgently. "Thank the Goddess, you're alright. What happened? Your tongue! And Dario came and ..." He stared over her shoulder, his expression baffled. "Who in hell are those two women and where did *they* come from?"

CHAPTER SIXTEEN

EMRYN

*E*mryn's grip on Lyssica's arms slackened enough for her to twist and see two females glowering over the Bodach's prone body. She heaved in a great breath; her exhale accompanied by a trill of delight. As her voice lilted through the air, both females turned their heads; the younger lady's smile lighting her face with incandescent pleasure.

"Lyssica!"

The older one simply nodded. She was white of skin and hair, with one grey eye and the other a brightly gleaming white. Those mismatched eyes were narrowed, her blood-red mouth pursed as she returned to studying the Bodach, motionless at her feet. Printed with all types of small white skulls, her dark red robe brushed the muddy ground; a small set of deer antlers separated the long snowy hair clipped back from her face with barrettes adorned by tiny, pointy snouted, animal skulls.

The younger female was gowned in a cream-etched satin dress, gathered close to her torso by a green corset. Her full skirts swept the leaf litter and broken snow of the forest floor but showed no evidence of being wet or stained. A full length, voluminous green velvet cloak, dotted with small purple blossoms, hung behind her shoulders but still managed to flow around and over the sides of her skirts in queen-like glory. Her luminous creamy skin, coupled with green eyes and long, wavy, golden hair, bearing a wreath of colourful blossoms and leaves, gave her ethereal beauty an eldritch radiance.

Emryn forgot to blink as this glowing vision drifted towards them. The lady's robe trailed across the ground, light welling around her like sunshine dispersing clouds. Her every step shed tiny flowers which took root as if they'd always been there. Reaching them, she gathered Lyssica into her arms, hugging and rocking her. Lyssica sighed and relaxed. Over her head the Lady's gaze swept Emryn in a brief assessment, leaving him feeling weighed and measured down to his very soul. Despite that, he didn't feel threatened.

Kynthcat's paws batted softly. *'She see me, too! Who she is?'*

The lady smiled, but her focus dropped to the Fae-female she held. "Lyssica, beloved child. I'm so pleased to see you well."

Emryn shook off his stupefaction, satisfied that this female meant Lyssica no harm. *'Don't know. Looks like I imagine a goddess would.'* The crone moved, drawing his attention – he wasn't so sure about her. She'd stooped to place her hands either side of the Bodach's temples and was muttering a constant, unintelligible litany of soft voiced sound. She stayed so for several moments, then straightened with a harsh grimace and followed in Ostara's footsteps.

Kynthcat grumbled, snarling unhappily. *'That evil creature dead? He should be.'*

'Doubt it.'

'He harmed our mate.'

'And she kicked his arse.'

A chuff. *'Ha! You not deny this time!'*

Grief over the insurmountable situation filled Emryn; why was Kynthcat persisting with the impossibility of this mate business when it couldn't possibly be true? Even if he wished it was with every fibre of his being. To find such a one as Lyssica and have to give her up, lose her—

A shake to his shoulder dragged him from his misery. Personal flame now quenched, Dario loomed over him. "Ready to stand?" Without awaiting an answer, he stooped, positioned a shoulder under Emryn's armpit and hoisted. The action drew the attention of all three women. Ostara tilted her head.

"Lyssica could you introduce us to these delightful Fae-males?"

She beamed delightedly, but Emryn's heart hurt as she opened her mouth, then froze and let it fall shut. Her face filled with pain. Parting her lips, she uttered a hoarse noise and indicated her lack of tongue with one finger.

Ostara peered in, then frowned. "Tut, tut. We can't have that." She glanced back at her companion. "Cailli, your consort's worked overtime here." She placed one hand on the side of Lyssica's neck and the other high on her throat. Growling, the hag placed one hand atop Ostara's at throat position and her second on the opposite side of Lyssica's neck. Both ladies' hands glowed; Ostara's with green-gold light and the hag's a pearlescent white. The Goddess of Spring nodded at the crone beside her. "By the way, this lovely lady with me is the Cailleach. Cailleach meet Lyssica."

"And ye were right, young Lyssica." The hag's voice was soft as snow. "I've no wish to be saddled with permanent winter. My Bo wasn't using his brains for their true purpose." Her red lips peeled back to expose bare gums. "Nice of him to plan a gift, although ..." She shook her head, the smile fading. "I don't endorse any of his methods and so I'll tell him." Her mismatched eyes swept over them; the white one ice-crystal sharp, the grey as threatening as a winter storm. "I offer my sincerest apologies for the actions of my consort." She withdrew her hand from atop Ostara's and let the other fall from Lyssica's neck. Her voice emerged gratingly harsh and blizzard cold. "Because he meddled and instigated an early winter, I will end the season early. I also grant the three of ye, plus all people and things connected to ye, my full protection – my Bo can be mean when he's thwarted.

Granted, I sent him to stand in for me when we goddesses decided on a meeting, but it wasn't to behave as he did and his reports to me did not paint a true picture, else I would've been here to stop him."

Running her hand down Lyssica's throat, Ostara tapped the centre of the clavicle then drew her hand away. "Try now, my dear."

Eyes round, Lyssica's fingers rose to her lips while she switched her gaze from Ostara, to the Cailleach, to Dario and finally to Emryn. "M-my tongue." A smile dawned. "It's regrown. I'm talking!"

Dario grinned. "Even the blood is gone,"

Emryn drank in her flushed and happy face. "Thank the Sands of Time!" Unable to resist, his hand cupping her cheek, he bent to kiss the temptation of her pretty mouth. Her lips flowered beneath his, clinging in full participation.

Next to Emryn, Dario cleared his throat. "My pardon, High Ladies of the Year's Cycle, but since Lyssica is, again, temporarily mute, permit me to introduce myself. Dario Eribifax, Duke of Garadenya at your service. And the person attached to Lyssica's mouth is Lord Emryn Phengaris, a beta Kynthcat of the Destrion Changeling Clan. It is our pleasure to meet such illustrious goddesses." He swept a deep bow.

Parting from Lyssica, Emryn slid his hand down to grip hers then bowed. "Dear Goddesses, my thanks for assisting Lyssica to regain her tongue, although I will not apologise for my distraction."

Inside him, Kynthcat preened. *'A mate shouldn't have to.'*

Ostara nodded. "She is dear to you then?"

He nodded. "She is an unexpected delight I would never have found without the winter exchange program instigated by the United Queendom of the Fae Demesnes." He sighed, spoke deliberately, as much for the goddesses as in warning to Kynthcat. "It is sad that our time together will end in just over in a week at the program's conclusion."

Ostara's gaze sharpened; she took note of Lyssica glancing

away towards the forest. "You will leave?"

"I'd love to stay here and build a life with Lyssica." He cast her a beseeching look. "I *want* to stay." The corners of Emryn's mouth turned down. "But changelings are tethered to their Alpha and the pack; thus, we cannot be away for too long and because we *are* pack animals, we cannot break our tethers without becoming feral or mad. I have no choice but to return to my pack, like it or not." He glanced between Dario and Lyssica. "It has been a wonderful visit, and I hate even the thought of leaving." He swallowed, glanced from Lyssica to Dario and back. "I would really like permission to return."

'I tell you we find our mate and you call it interesting visit?' A snarl reverberated through his chest; he sucked in a hard breath as claws scored and slashed inside him. He gritted his teeth.

'I keep telling you – she can't be our mate, however much we'd like her to be – she's not changeling. I'd be overjoyed if she were. I love her and want to be with her regardless of that.'

His expression serious, Dario nodded. "We have enjoyed your visit also. Come back any time, Emryn."

Even though Lyssica smiled, the stretch of her mouth trembled with sadness. "You'll always be welcome, Emryn. We have worked together so well; your help has been invaluable and … and I care for you." The deep wells of her eyes shone with a combination of tears and love. Emryn clenched his fists and dropped his head. She loved him, just as he loved her.

"A fitting finish." The Cailleach clapped her hands, breaking the melancholy of the moment. "Ostara, I formally hand the seasonal reigns over to ye. May I have my potion?"

"My pleasure, Cailli." Reaching into her cloak, Ostara produced a small leather flask, waved her hand over it, then held it out. Taking the flask, the Cailleach unstoppered it and drank the contents in one continuous mouthful. She shuddered as she re-stoppered the empty container and returned it, then stiffened and closed her eyes as her face spasmed. Before the astonished gaze of all but Ostara, the Cailleach continued to spasm and shudder as her face and body changed from crone to middle aged matron, to young woman. She coughed, then her eyes re-opened.

"Thank ye Ostara. Wonderful to share time with ye, as always." She reached to touch Lyssica on the shoulder. "And I thank ye for all the hard work ye've put in, my dear, and for not giving up. Ye are a credit to yer line." She gave the males a smile and a nod, before tramping forcefully back to where the Bodach still lay. Bending, she touched a forefinger to the centre of his forehead, the hollow at the base of his throat and the place above his heart, muttering all the while, then she straightened, placing her hands on her hips. The Bodach began to stir immediately, arms and legs twitching. His head tilted, then he sighted the woman standing over him and stilled.

His gravelly voice carried to them. "Cailli, my dearest. You're here. A little early, but—"

She pointed a finger at him. "Be quiet, Bo. I know what ye've been doing and I'm not happy."

"Dear One, it was meant to be a gift."

She smacked her fist into her other hand. "No! I've no wish to work full time, to be forever old, to have no surcease. Ostara's Lady Lyssica tried to tell ye that – ye should've listened. Although by then all yer damage had been done." She glowered at him. "All the harm ye've caused, the blood ye've shed, aligning yerself with evil and death magic – what were ye thinking?"

"But Dear One, you are aligned with destruction—"

"Ye know it is something I *never* use lightly and then only after I've exhausted my options. And ..." She pointed again, her expression fiercely forbidding. "As the patroness of starving wolves, how dare ye align with the Vulpia breed? How double damn dare ye!"

"But Cailli, my dear—"

The Cailleach gave an exclamation of distaste, reached down, clasped a wrist and jerked him upright. "Life, and the respect of it, is a part of my work – am I not also a professional deer-herder? I cannot tell ye how disgusted I am with what ye've done here." Hand rising, she pinched his earlobe and started walking, ensuring he must follow or risk having the lobe ripped off. Follow he did, head on one side, voice raised in protest, his steps staggering as the Cailleach dragged him away. Eight steps later, a ground mist rose around their legs, wreathed their bodies, climbing up and up until they were obscured from view. Their voices, one protesting, the other angry, faded and when the mist cleared, the two were gone.

Ostara's laugh tinkled. "He will not dare set a foot wrong for a very long time."

Emryn snorted. "And that's it? All this death and destruction, and that's all? Forgive me if my sense of humour isn't the least bit tickled, Goddess."

Her expression sobered. "You are right, of course. Nothing he did is the least bit humorous – it is his immediate future which I find so amusing." She considered him. "And, no – that's not all. Lyssica nearly died, as did you. She healed you with the power I was finally able to despatch." She rubbed an eyebrow. "To my regret, I hadn't tried to check in – Lyssica's never had trouble before or been unable to contact me as necessary. I've always had full trust in her abilities."

Emryn spread his hands. "Yet, as a Handmaiden, her power and skills weren't even in the same league as those of the Bodach."

Ostara frowned. "He's the consort of a goddess, which makes him a Demigod with greater skills, but there was no way to anticipate his actions."

"And if he comes back?"

"He won't."

Dario stirred. "What if he seeks revenge? He's that type of personality, is he not?"

"He is." Ostara waved a hand in the direction of where they'd last seen the Cailleach and her spouse. "But, if you recall, the Cailleach put the three of you under her protection. You'll also be under my protection. You *will* be safe from reprisals. And now, Lord Emryn, I wish to give you a little power boost, which will ensure your full recovery. Is that agreeable to you?"

Conscious of Lyssica clutching his arm, eying him a trifle

anxiously, Emryn didn't protest. "I accept, thank you." Ostara pressed a palm to each temple and began to hum. He gasped as a jolt of raw energy coursed into him, eyes shooting wide. He'd been healing faster after Lyssica's touch, but now an intense blizzard of raw power zapped through every part of his body and although it healed him, he had the sense that Ostara had weighed and measured his physical make-up, his worth and his character, all at the same time.

He sagged as she removed her hands. Lyssica and Dario each grabbed an arm, supporting him. Blinking owlishly, he stared at the goddess. "That was fierce. Was I suffering so much injury?"

Ostara considered him, green eyes lambent, skin glowing golden. "A few things needed sorting; you'll do fine, now." She turned to Lyssica, who was bouncing from foot to foot. "Ah, still juiced up. We need a private conversation, my dear. We've some goddessy things to work through. Let's step over to the last stone in my circle."

Lyssica smiled. "Of course, my Lady."

"Wait!" Emryn's body trembled. "I feel strange. Are you certain I'm okay?"

One corner of her lips lifting, Ostara nodded. "Absolutely, Lord Emryn. As perfect, as can be. Just exactly what you need to be, in fact."

CHAPTER SEVENTEEN

LYSSICA

*T*he last stone in the circle was not particularly high, but it stood furthest away from the males. Ostara smoothed Lyssica's hair back from her face. At the goddess's touch, the tingling in Lyssica's skin increased, as though she were primed to explode in a shower of sparkles. Fighting to hold the euphoria in, she focused on the goddess's words.

"Your male has enhanced hearing due to his changeling heritage so I've also enclosed us in a privacy bubble. What I have to tell you is *your* information. You may decide to keep it private, but you're at liberty to share with whomever you wish, although I'd choose those folk carefully." Ostara scanned Lyssica's face, her own illuminated with the joy of life. "You've done a superlative job, dear one, succeeding against all odds."

Lyssica grinned, her insides bubbling, almost overflowing with her joy and delight. "Only because I was finally able to break through the barrier to reach you." She tilted her head. "I don't understand why we were disconnected. Do you know the cause?"

"Aye." Ostara grimaced. "The Bodach placed a veil between us. It was subtly done and my attention was on the other goddesses attending our meeting, so I didn't notice. He chose his time well, but then, his actions were all cleverly planned."

Lyssica rocked on the balls of her feet, a smile of happiness lighting her features. "I'm so pleased I finally broke through." Why did she feel like she wanted to sing at the top of her lungs and dance until she dropped with exhaustion?

Ostara pursed her lips as she considered Lyssica. "Let's hope you still think so after what I've to tell you." She reached out to clasp both of Lyssica's hands. "When you reached me and I was able to see, through your mind and memories, what was being perpetrated by the Bodach, I blasted you with the force you needed to resist, to fight back and overcome the Bodach. In so doing I had no choice but to use my power to change you into a being strong enough to contain and manage the sheer amount of magic I was pouring into you."

Lyssica stared uncomprehendingly, fighting to hold down the effervescence inside her. "But I'm your Handmaiden. I have been for years."

"Yes, that's true." Ostara's hands gripped more tightly as Lyssica jigged up and down. "But, as my Handmaiden, you already contained as much of my power as you could hold, in your current form. To give you what you needed to triumph, I had to make you more."

Lyssica gulped. "In what way?" The hairs on her body stood on end. "How much more?"

"You had to become enough to overcome the Bodach."

"B-but he … he's a Demigod! He told me; bragged about it."

"He is." Ostara nibbled on her bottom lip. "Although The Cail-leach has now placed a cap on his abilities in an effort to leash him somewhat."

"Oh." Lyssica tried to keep her feet still. "So, that makes me …"

"A Demigoddess."

"Ahh … I beg your pardon?" Lyssica paled, gaping, her eyes searching the emerald of Ostara's. A force inside her threatened to explode and shower the clearing with … what?

146

The goddess massaged Lyssica's fingers. "In fact, you are now a Demigoddess of Spring with a huge amount of magic, and the talent to take in more, from me or nature, as you need it. Plus, between us we've a more direct link which no-one but I can separate, or veil, as the Bodach did."

Sagging against the tor, Lyssica struggled against the incandescence threatening to burst from her, even as she took in the news. "Umm. I feel ..."

Ostara nodded. "Yes. You're awash with power while your body is adjusting to its new form. It will settle in a few days. In the meantime, you will be bubbling over with life, love and growth, shedding it in sparkles." The goddess patted her hand. "You'll be a veritable blizzard of joy and new beginnings for all those with whom you come in contact. It will help them through the terrible events brought about by the Bodach and usher them into a new, prosperous and rosy future. Do you understand, Lyssica, my daughter?"

"I-I think so." Lyssica licked her lips. "D-daughter?"

Ostara smiled. "Yes, indeed. With what I've done to you, it is as though you were born to me in the real sense; you're a piece of me."

"B-but ..."

Shaking her head, Ostara held up a hand. "It's okay. I don't wish to supplant your birth mother, Lyssica. Just think of me as your Fairy Goddess-mother, for in effect, that's what I am."

Quaking with the effort of holding the effervescence in, Lyssica managed a jerky nod. She swallowed and forced herself to say, "Okay Goddess-ma, I understand. I think."

A tinkle of laughter left Ostara's lips. "Goddess-ma. I like it." Her features softened. "Everything will settle and come right, you'll see." She sighed. "But now I must go, dear daughter. Although, I'll definitely be back. You're a delight to my ages-wearied senses." She leaned forward and kissed Lyssica's brow, waved at Emryn and Dario, who'd not taken their eyes off them, then vanished in a rainbow of green, gold and purple sparkles.

～

"Well, Trey and I disarmed every Vulpia attack-web we could find, but we didn't see any Vulpiawolves." Lyssica turned at the sound of Zhulija's voice, watched as Treymeron followed Zhulija into the circle, then sped to them on energy-winged feet.

"That's because they were all here!" Lyssica hugged Zhulija, then moved to hug Treymeron as well. The neck of his jerkin wriggled and a baby duskit peeked out. He reared back.

"Don't squash Pinkerpush!"

"Okay, okay." Her hands came out, palms facing him in a warding gesture. "Wasn't aware you still had this little one – why do you?"

A sheepish expression flitted across his face. "She won't leave me. The three Papan has won't be parted from him either. It's like they form an emotional attachment somehow." Then, he scowled at her. "What's with you? You're bouncing like you're on jump juice and blow me down if you didn't just leave a trail of sparkling glittery stuff as you ran to us."

"Ooh, did I really?" Lyssica pranced in a circle trying to see the effect, which drew the attention of everyone else. "Ostara said I might do that." She giggled.

Dario raised an eyebrow. "You sound as if you're tipsy as all hell."

Emryn growled. "You're raining glittery stuff – what did Ostara do to you?"

She waved an airy hand. "Just a little overflow of the magic she shared to overcome the bad folk." Rising to her toes, she spun in a circle, spreading more tiny shimmer particles. "No nasties left now."

Treymeron scowled, gestured to the body of Perris. "Well, he's nasty and he's still here."

Grimacing briefly, Lyssica cast a look at the prone body. "We probably should check, but the devil-rabbit ripped his throat out, so he's more than likely dead."

"Oh!" Treymeron pursed his lips. "Well, I know I should say it's a terrible thing, but after what he did to you?" He shook his head. "I can't."

"The devil-rabbit was here?" Emryn stiffened. "What happened? Where'd he go?" He scanned the surrounding woods intently.

"I took care of him." Lyssica couldn't stop shifting from foot to foot as she brought everyone who hadn't been present, up to date. "And as for the Vulpiawolves, Cailleach took them when she dragged the Bodach off." Lyssica grinned pirouetting and causing a rainbow of tiny fireglows.

"I want to hear exactly what happened." Dario cleared his throat. "But probably best to wait until we're with everyone so you don't have to repeat it over and over. Plus, it's late and we must all get home."

Zhulija caught his arm. "Beloved, I believe it would be best if we all go back to Papillion for tonight – we've survived a fight, some of us are injured, we're all in need of winding down, especially Lyss, and it's the closest place."

Dario's fingers closed over her hand. "Excellent solution, my darling. Papillion it is."

"And I guess we should take you-know-who back." Treymeron jerked a thumb towards Perris.

Zhulija rolled her eyes. "Wow, Trey, your sensitivity is amazing."

He scowled. "He might be dead, but he's still a swine."

Emryn's voice rumbled dryly. "Maybe you could suggest that to his parents as an epitaph."

~

Thus, a strange cavalcade returned to the Papillion Estate. Kynthcat carried the body of Perris slung over his back. Treymeron, Zhulija and Dario flew, while Lyssica, still full of

149

boundless energy, danced along at Kynthcat's side. The fliers landed as they reached the gates of the estate.

Treymeron shook his head. "I don't know if anyone else noticed, but those sparks Lyss is spreading around are amaze-balls. Some become flowers immediately upon touching the ground and if they land on plants, there's an instant reanimation or growth spurt. She's full of go-go juice."

Zhulija turned and stared. "Goddess bless, you're right Trey! Look at all those little blossoms."

Lyssica did another glitter spreading pirouette and beamed. "Ostara said it will settle – eventually."

Dario shook his head. "Just as well one of us kept an eye out for danger." Zhulija blew him a kiss and his hand shot up to snatch it out of the air. She giggled as he made a show of raising the captured kiss to his lips.

Signing in at the guard house, they made their way to a shed at the back of the manor where they could lay Perris' body. By then, a crowd had gathered, both animals and Fae-folk, all drawn to Lyssica and the energy she radiated. She was thrilled to share, bless and coo, a repeat of her sessions in the forest. Later, she walked through the barns and stables, attending to creatures too ill or injured to move.

She shared the news wherever she went. "I'm happy to announce Ostara has made a deal with the Cailleach and the unnatural winter is over. The Vulpiawolves, devil-rabbit and the Bodach have gone, so conditions will improve over the next week or so. By Ostara's Day at the Spring Equinox, good weather conditions will be here." She stroked a quivering fox. "Of course, everyone may stay as long as they need or wish."

Zhulija tapped shoulder. "Lyss, it's time to clean up for dinner." She gazed at the fox. "Sorry little Reynard, but she must leave now." The fox uttered a soft 'yip', licked Lyssica's hand and laid his head down on the blanket.

Dinner was tumultuous. Lyssica couldn't sit still and the report of the forest fight had to be repeated several times. Everyone had queries, while the answers and explanations only gave rise to more questions.

Lyssica's parents, plus Kerrigold, Melkaz and Venaday all watched her in amazement. Emryn blew her a kiss, Zhulija winked, while Treymeron and Dario simply grinned as they watched everyone's reaction to the gyrations inspired by her excess of energy.

Duke Yanvian patted his mouth with a napkin, then fed tiny morsels of food to each of the three duskits in a basket at his feet. "So, Ostara filled you with enough power to take down the Bodach and now you have to wait for it to ease?"

Lyssica grinned. "That's correct, Papan." She danced at her plate, loaded her fork with food and popped it into her mouth.

"When will that happen?"

She shrugged. "No idea, Papan." She was keeping the truth quiet for now.

"Are you able to concentrate?" Her father eyed her searchingly. "There's something I wish to say."

Venaday wagged his finger. "It'd better be pleasant, your Grace. I want her in a good mood so she'll agree to be my consort."

Lyssica rolled her eyes. "Oh do give up, Venaday! There's no way I'll ever agree."

Duke Yanvian stood, glaring at Venaday. "And there's the first thing. You, Sir, will cease importuning my daughter for her hand. She's said 'no' more than once. Do you have a hearing problem?"

Venaday's mouth fell open. "B-but, you were the one who said she was available."

Zhulija's fingers went to her mouth. "Papan, you didn't!"

With both Lyssica and Duchesse Azura glaring at him, Yanvian reddened. "Unfortunately, I did, but I've come to realise the choice isn't up to me, never was, and it was wrong of me to imply other-wise." He met Lyssica's angry stare. "I'm sorry and I'm taking this chance to publicly apologise." He glanced around the table. "When

Lyss first broached the idea of learning estate management, I found it impossible to look at my beautiful daughter and see anything other than my little girl who loved tea parties and frilly things. To my regret I told her to go and be a traditional female, a brainless, pampered socialite."

He sighed. "I conceived a plan of finding a consort for her, but when DeMaksim's life took a new turn, I agreed to give Lyss a chance at being the heir." He cleared his throat and took a sip of water. "To my surprise and delight, I've discovered that Lyssica's skills at estate management are nothing short of brilliant. I've also come to know her as an adult, something which has brought me nothing but joy. I'm forced to confess how mistaken I was to pre-judge her as I did." He scanned the table of watchers again. "Don't get me wrong, the wonderful discovery of my daughter being fully capable of running this estate, probably any estate, has thrilled me no end." He smiled at Lyssica, then spread his hands, palms upward. "I looked in the mirror and saw a fool."

She had her fingers over her mouth as she watched him while bouncing on restless feet. His gaze softened.

"Furthermore, if she takes a consort, it will be her decision and choice of partner."

He walked around the table towards a stunned Lyssica and extended his arms. "My dearest Lyssica, I now see I've been blessed to have you as my daughter and I would be overjoyed if you can please forgive my stupidity."

Her voice trembled, a wobbly smile gracing her lips. "Oh Papan, how lovely. I do forgive you. Thank you." Accepting his hug, she grasped his shoulders and danced around the room, accompanied by their onlookers' laughter and applause. As she spun with her father, her gaze found Emryn, staring with pride and something looking suspiciously like the love which filled her heart to overflowing. Her soul bloomed in the joy of the night.

CHAPTER EIGHTEEN

EMRYN

$\mathcal{A}$t bedtime, Duchesse Azura, with Duke Yanvian in tow, sought Emryn out. "I've had the Peony Room prepared for you, Emryn." She smiled, then noticed Lyssica shaking her head.

"Something wrong, Lyss?"

"No, nothing is wrong." Lyssica spoke firmly. "But Emryn is sharing my room – we're in a relationship and have been for some weeks now."

Her mother cocked a knowing eyebrow. "Ah, I'd begun to suspect."

Duke Yanvian's brows snapped together. "In a relationship? That's not—" His Duchesse elbowed him. "Ah!" He visibly swallowed. "Um, would it be alright if I ask your reasons for such a choice? Considering our societal strictures?"

Emryn enclosed Lyssica's hand in one of his as she wet her lips. "Well Papan, during that party period we both now regret, something happened to alter my perception of life and those societal strictures you mentioned."

Yanvian's gaze sharpened. "Go on."

Lyssica forged on. "An unscrupulous bastard – you know him as Perris Momphiday – drugged me to insensibility then had his way with me." Her parents drew in harsh, shocked breaths. "I was uncomfortable talking about the event, at the time. I-I wasn't in a good place. I admit it was a hard path to walk alone, but I learned to value myself as more than a precept of imposed beliefs." Her fist pressed her chest. "At my core, I'm still the same Lyssica, regardless of the rules and behaviours of others. I've learned to listen to my instincts, do what I believe is right – since obeying the advice of others meant I didn't like who I was and left me in a horrible situation."

Releasing his grip on her hand, Emryn wrapped an arm around her; he was solidly in her corner, sick at the harm she'd endured. Too bad that bastard, Momphiday, was already dead. Then, Treymeron appeared beside him, Zhulija and Dario planting themselves on Lyssica's other side and the support settled him, warming his core. Glancing around, Lyssica identified her siblings' support; a smile curved her lips.

'Our female very brave.' Kynthcat preened.

Lyssica's body expanded on a deep breath. "Emryn and I were drawn to each other from the beginning. We acknowledged it and I—" She turned to Emryn, gaze tender. He smiled at her as she continued. "I needed the power to choose for myself, since such a selection had previously been torn from my grasp. I wanted the liberty to connect with someone on my terms – doing so has done wonders for my self-esteem." Her gaze returned to her parents. "I'll apologise to no-one for my choices. However, I understand if you find this reality difficult."

Duchesse Azura's eyes shone with tears. "Oh, my dearest Lyss! That you endured that terrible experience alone. I'm so sorry you didn't find us approachable. I told Yanvian I disagreed with his stance, but I wanted you both to find solutions without my intervention. What an awful mistake!" She held out her arms. "May I hug you?"

"Of course, Maman." Sagging with relief, Lyssica stepped out of Emryn's embrace and into her mother's. Beside them, the duke quivered with fury. Emryn waited for his explosion – would he refuse to acknowledge his blame in the matter and turn on Lyssica again?

"I can't believe this!" Yanvian's eyes were wild with bitter fury. "Momphiday?! How dare he! The nerve – coming here a program applicant, forcing his company on you after he'd … he'd … If he weren't already dead, I'd rip his man parts off and feed them to him. That no-good, lying, disgusting vart-demon! I just can't—" He broke off, hands clutching his hair. A harsh sob tore from him, the shards of sorrow in the sound almost tangible. Lyssica moved from her mother's arms to hug him.

"Oh, Papan."

His arms encircled her. "Oh, my sweet girl. Can you ever forgive me?"

Lyssica rocked him. "You didn't do it, Papan."

"No, but I manipulated you into a position where a predator hurt you." A tear trickled down the side of his nose. "I don't think I can forgive myself. I was a rigid, rule-structured fool and see where it's gotten us?"

"Shh, Papan. Shh. As I told Emryn, Zhu and Dario, I'm now telling you – I've come to terms with it. Yes the events were terrible, but I survived and I've come out the other side a stronger Fae-female. I like who I am. Do you hear me?"

He drew back a little. "I'm proud of you, daughter. So proud. You're wonderful and I support your right to choose anything in your life." Eyes wet, he looked directly at Emryn, then his mouth firmed and he nodded.

"You've picked a beautiful Fae-lady to share this visit with."

Emryn seized the opening. "I plan to spend a lot more than just my visit with Lyss."

Yanvian looked taken aback. "But you … you're leaving soon. Aren't you?"

"I am." Emryn confirmed. "Pack tethering means I don't have a choice, as I've discussed with Lyssica previously, but I'm coming back." He focused on his love. "I'm definitely coming back. My Kynthcat declared Lyssica our mate from the beginning."

Lyssica gasped. "He did?"

"Yes. But fool me … I was uncertain because there's never been a mating to someone outside the pack." He turned to face her father. "But I no longer care. I love Lyssica." He met her startled, overjoyed gaze. "Yes, you." His finger touched the tip of her nose as she stood within her father's grasp. "I love you Lyssica Aphiski." Tender warmth filled his smile. "I love you and wish to spend my life with you, however we can arrange it. What do you say?"

"Yes. I say yes!" Lyssica released her father and leaped towards him. He caught her, pulling her close, his breath catching as the heat of her gaze thrilled him and Kynthcat to their core. "My Emryn Kynthcat, I'm so in love with you, so very much. You're my every wish and dream made real and I'm keeping you."

He kissed her then, regardless of the onlookers, the hooting, the whistling, the applause. He kissed her with all of the love in his soul.

'Maybe not so stupid after all.' Kynthcat did a jiggy, bucking prance, purring with happiness.

After a while, Emryn drew back, looking for Lyssica's parents. He was pleased to see them smiling, their arms around each other.

Unable to bow while clutching Lyssica, Emryn nodded his head to them. "Your Graces, I seek your blessing. I'd like to talk with you about what I can offer Lyssica and, by extension, your family, but to do that I must travel back to my pack and sort matters out with my family. I need my Alpha's help and guidance about the best way forward. I know there's a week left of the program, since the contract was to end on Ostara's Day at Spring Equinox, but I'd like permission to leave tomorrow."

"Permission granted." Dario said, smiling just as widely as his mate.

"Thank you." He turned to everyone then to say, "Know, all of you, and bear witness. I vow myself bound to Lyssica Aphiski." He raised her hands to his lips, kissed her knuckles, met her shining eyes. "I promise you, I will return as soon as I can organise every-thing, but I'd be remiss if I didn't explain: the details could take several weeks. It'll be difficult without you, my love, but I seek to construct our future."

She stretched on tiptoes to kiss him, a brief, but sound meeting of their mouths, leaving him hungry for more. "I understand." Relieved, he hugged her. Over her head, her parents still smiled. Euphoria blossomed within him and Kynthcat batted imaginary hearts and flowers.

'*Like kissing. More of that.*' The large, twin horned, furry animal attempted to pucker his mouth, to make kiss lips.

Emryn choked on a cough, but didn't miss Duke Yanvian's extended forearm, the Fae-warriors' recognition of equals. He accepted gratefully; then watched a look of wonder and delight bloom on Lyssica's face as Yanvian offered his forearm to her. "Oh!" Slowly, she responded, her gaze scanning her father's features.

"I acknowledge you, Lyssica, in your own right – as your Father, I give my blessing to you both."

"As do I." Duchesse Azura reached out to hug all three of them, something which culminated in a mother-daughter embrace, as the two Fae-males eased aside.

Emryn and Yanvian eyed one another. Yanvian's mouth twisted. "Hidebound as I am by the old ways, I can't say this any other way. After coming to know you during this program, I'm more than pleased to pass my daughter and her care into your safekeeping."

"I accept in the spirit of the offer." This time Emryn did bow. "In my clan, I'm a beta Kynthcat, but not because I'm weak. It simply means I'm rock solid in support and protection of my Alpha. That's how my role with Lyssica will work. If she asks me, I'll suggest, maybe advise and we'll discuss options, but ultimately, I'll always have her back, no matter her choices. You understand?"

Yanvian returned the bow. "I do. Now that I have shrugged off the veil of my idiocy, I see how perfect you are for my daughter and I'm well content."

The night was an explosion of love and joy. Emryn could keep neither lips nor hands from Lyssica's glowing, delectable body and she was equally as eager for him, overflowing with energy and joy. She'd confessed her new Demigoddess status to him, but it changed nothing – she'd been his goddess from the second she'd toppled into his arms at the welcome dinner.

Roused in the early light of dawn by Lyssica kissing and licking her way across his pecs and up to his neck, he drew her close.

"I adore your aroma, Emryn." Her voice was throaty and he smiled, fondly remembering the delighted screams he'd caused during their loving.

"And I, yours, my darling; your scent is home." He stroked the curve of her spine until he reached the swell of her bottom. Grasping the curves with both hands, he urged her to sit astride him – not for the first time. He adored seeing his Lyssica take what she wanted from him – a victory for them both.

She sighed delightedly as he surged up inside her. She was amazing, as was her delectable heat, the feeling of being snugly home within her; those sensations would draw him forever. Nothing, nobody, had ever felt so wonderful. Her hands were on his chest, massaging, digging fingernails in – once she grasped how much he loved the prick of fingernails, the sharp bite of her teeth, she didn't hold back. They'd discovered she enjoyed being bitten by him too; but was a little wary of his claws – after all, Kynthcat's were a heck of a lot sharper.

'Me never hurt our mate.' Kynthcat purred, wallowing in the sensations rolling through them.

'I know. She'll learn.'

Lyssica stilled suddenly, her fingers grazing a tender spot on his neck. "Your skin's broken there." Her eyes sought his. "I-I think I drew blood, Emryn."

He grinned. "Oh, I know you did. It was wonderful, mate."

"Am I?" Her brow furrowed. "Are we really mates? Being from two different cultures and all?"

His grin widened. "Oh yes, you'll see when I return the favour. We might be from separate cultures, but both of those are still Fae. I know your branch has some other rituals, but for us, sex, biting and blood are the sealers. Although I'll dance your Rhynfallia with you whenever you want."

"Hmm." The frown cleared. She swept her hair back behind one gorgeously pointed ear. "May I ask, what you're waiting for then?"

"Nothing." Without warning, he eased her torso forward, one hand fisted her hair and he sank fangs into the glowing tawny skin of her throat. The hard thrust of his cock into her sex, the rough upward pumping of his hips, catapulted them both sky-high. Emryn's vision whited out at the combined sensations of their mutual orgasm, the drops of Lyssica's blood sliding sweetly into his system. His guttural roar was matched by her cry as their mating bond snapped into place, coursing through their bodies with the force of a winter blizzard being blown away by the cyclonic beginnings of spring.

CHAPTER NINETEEN

LYSSICA

*H*e'd been gone a day over four weeks and Lyssica missed Emryn so fiercely she felt sick. Taking a sip of hot, fortifying tea, she stared at her breakfast morosely. Surely he'd be back soon?

The rumble of her father's voice drew Lyssica's attention.

"Azura, are you alright?" Papan's brow furrowed as he watched his consort poke at a slice of toast. "You usually have eggs as well."

Duchesse Azura smiled at him. "I'm fine, Yanvian, my love." She nibbled an edge of her toast. His frown lightened, but he continued to watch. She chewed and swallowed. "I just feel like plain toast this morning."

Still sipping her tea, Lyssica absently observed their interchange. Ever since she'd received the massive energy charge from Ostara, the estate and surrounds were bursting with the new season's light and warmth.

The Spring Equinox had become a festival of joy and love; animals and Fae all mingling fearlessly while honouring Ostara, the Goddess of Spring, Fertility and New Beginnings. Ostara had graced them with Her presence, hugging Lyssica and kissing her on both cheeks in front of everyone. The action, normally something shared between family members, brought Lyssica a recognition she hadn't been fully prepared for. So many animals flocked to her, she was in danger of tripping over them; Fae couples approached for her blessing – one she happily provided, despite how self-conscious the focus felt.

Still radiant with the magic Ostara had shared, she continued to leave a trail of sparkles and tiny blossoms. After overcoming her embarrassment at everyone's fascination with the phenomenon, it became fun to finger-flick the glitter of her new power over everyone who approached, to watch them glow with pleasure as shimmers and flowers enveloped them. To her secret delight, she could see the magic sink deep into their bodies; watch them heal from tiny maladies of flesh and spirit they'd previously taken in stride; and see them come alive with new energy.

But was it ethical to perform internal checks on folk if they weren't expecting it? Perhaps she should do it openly. Maybe she could offer a healing and helping clinic for a few hours weekly, open to anyone, with some folk specifically invited? She chewed her toast as she thought about it, finally deciding it was a good idea. For now, though, there was Maman to consider.

"Maman? Would you allow me to scan you? Make certain you're well?"

A warm smile lit the Duchesse's face. "Of course, Lyss. I'd love to be your practice partner."

Returning the smile, Lyssica assessed her mother through her screen of enhanced power. To her elation, the source of the discomfort was easily located, but the reason, oh, that reason ... She covered her lips with her fingertips, staring at her mother while contemplating the miracle she'd seen. Did Maman know?

"Well? Just tell me the issue, Lyssica. There's no need to blink at me like a stunned fallow deer."

"Um, Maman—" She scanned again, just to be sure.

The Duchesse rolled her eyes. "You did another magical inspection, didn't you?"

"Um, yes."

Azura sighed, smiling indulgently. "I suppose we'll get used to your new skills, but it'll take a while." She tipped her head to the side. "Did you find anything wrong?"

Lyssica smiled weakly. "Well, no. Nothing wrong. Per se. It's just ..."

Her mother stilled. "Just what?"

Lyssica cleared her throat. "You're expecting a baby." There was a brief, charged silence before Duke Yanvian leapt to his feet.

"What?!"

Maman's mouth had fallen open. She snapped it shut, staring wide-eyed at her toast. "Oh." She rolled her lips in and out, her gaze rising to meet Lyssica's. "Of course. My change of appetite, the way I ... Yes, it makes sense now." She swallowed, her face paler than earlier. "You sensed, or saw, the differences in me?"

Lyssica tilted her hand from side to side. "Well, yes, but I can also sense and see the baby."

"Baby?" Suddenly Treymeron's head shot up, the conversation having broken the barrier of his concentration. His fingers clamped the book he'd been reading. "There's a baby? We're going to have a new brother or sister?"

"Yes." Lyssica grinned.

A heavy thump emanated from her father's direction, but when Lyssica looked, she couldn't see him. She frowned. "Where's Papan?"

"On the floor." Duchesse Azura giggled, then covered her mouth with a trembling hand. "I think he passed out."

Everywhere she went that day, Lyssica recognised the same state in many females at Papillion, be they Fae or animal. There were plenty of new pregnancies. She was stunned. Still in the barn with some of the recovering fauna, she somewhat nervously communed with Ostara.

'Goddess-ma, there's a blessing of new babies on the way.'

A wash of love flowed across the link. 'Lyssica, my dear. Yes, it's common in spring.'

'I know, but there seems to be a lot. I mean, more than usual.'

'An overflow from you, dear one.' Amusement came. 'You've been spreading the power widely, haven't you?'

'Well, yes, Goddess-ma, but—'

'Lyssica, we're fertility goddesses, remember?'

'Oh. Yes.'

'Although the mother does have to indulge in some lovemaking with her mate or consort – doesn't she?'

'Lovemaking with her ...' Suddenly, Lyssica was overcome by an urge to sit down. Muscles quivering, mouth dry, she checked, and gasped. Blindly, she reached out to grip some nearby railing.

'Holy Mother Goddess, I'm pregnant!'

'Congratulations, my dear Lyssica.'

'You knew!'

Ostara corrected her. 'I knew it would happen. It was quite inevitable with the combination of a new mate and your power flux.'

'You could've have warned me.'

A tinkle of laughter. 'Would it have changed anything? Our magic is strong enough to realign female cycles – it's who we are.'

Lyssica gulped. 'Are you saying I'm destined to be pregnant for the rest of my life?'

More laughter. 'Only if you want that. As your magic settles and you discover more about it, you'll learn to fine tune and only be fertile when you wish it. Right now though, the huge influx meant you avoiding pregnancy was like a fish attempting to swim against an extremely strong current.'

'Little chance of success?' Lyssica massaged her temples.

'Not with an earthy new mate.'

⁓

Emryn deserved to be first to know their news, so Lyssica tried to appear as she usually did. With the spotlight heavily on her mother, it wasn't as difficult as she'd imagined.

Duchesse Azura twisted her fingers together as she paced the library. "I've seven adult children; I thought I was well past the time of bearing offspring."

From his reclining position on a window seat, Duke Yanvian shook his head. He wore a drunken expression of wondrous joy, despite having tossed back only one small, celebratory beaker of flamuisge.

"A baby at our age; it's a blessing I still can't believe." One of his three little duskit shadows chirruped softly, climbed his leg and scampered into the curve of his neck. To Lyssica's amusement, it snuggled in, mewing and patting him with one tiny paw.

A faint chuckle reached her; she turned, taking in Treymeron, sprawled on a second window seat, gently stroking the infant duskit on his chest with one long finger.

Lyssica sniggered. "Obviously, neither you nor Maman are too old and you're getting heaps of excellent practice with those duskit babies." Her hand wave encompassed both Fae-males. "They seem to have formed some sort of bond with both you and Trey – you're already surrogate mothers."

Spearing her with wide eyes, Treymeron clutched Pinkerpush firmly, but shook his head. "I'm no-one's mother!"

She snorted. "Okay, a father then, but you're still parenting her."

"Lyss's right, Trey," Duke Yanvian continued to watch his consort who was mumbling as she finger counted. When she stopped at the second last digit and gazed at him almost helplessly, he nodded.

"It's okay, my lovely one. When are we due?"

Azura smiled weakly. "I think, late in the Moon of Mayember."

Lyssica clapped her hands. "How wonderful!" *Oh, goody, a blessing of new babies at the end of Autumn – at the moment only I know just how wonderfully momentous that's going to be.*

A ruckus drifted from the front hall. Both Yanvian and Treymeron sat up, focusing on the outer door, just as a knock sounded. It opened. Entanglit appeared and bowed. "The Duke and Duchesse of Garadenya with guests, your Graces."

Zhulija burst in, radiating excitement; Dario followed closely, hand outstretched.

"Have a care, sweeting. Please?"

Treymeron's groan was heartfelt. "By the Goddess, Zhu! Don't tell me you're pregnant too?"

She stopped short, face falling. "What? Yes, I am. What's wrong with you, Trey? Aren't you thrilled for me? For us?" She waved blindly at Dario.

"Yeah, yeah, sorry – it's just that we're surrounded by fertile females apparently. It's exciting, but a little disconcerting, having everyone fall pregnant at the same time."

Zhulija stared first at her mother, then at her sister, then back to her brother. Beside her, Dario guided her further into the room. "Everyone? What do you mean, Trey? Lyss. Are you expecting too?"

"No, not her." Treymeron's blithe comment took the pressure off Lyssica. "But Maman, some other estate females and many of the animals."

"Maman?!" Zhulija's squeal was deafening. "Oh Maman, that's wonderful."

Dario glared at Treymeron. "I'm certain I heard you congratulating us just now, didn't I?"

Treymeron surged to stand, Pinkerpush vanishing inside the neck of his shirt. "Oh! Oh, absolutely! It's marvellous. Congratulations Zhu and you too, Dario!"

From the doorway, Entanglit coughed. "Excuse me, but I'd like to introduce Alpha Kynth-lord Bregal Phengaris, his mate Kynth-lady Renfa Urlnyth-Phengaris and their sons, Kynth-lords Delano, Tucker and Emryn Phengaris."

There was a bevy of excited greeting, to which Lyssica was

oblivious as, incandescent with joy, she ran for Emryn. Equally as intent, he was half way across the room to meet her.

"Lyss, my beloved!"

"My Emryn, thank goodness!" Heedless of everyone in the room, they embraced passionately. The familiar feel of Emryn's large warm hand cupping the nape of her neck, while his other clutched her close and tight, heated an internal pit Lyssica hadn't realised was cold. Emryn was here – he'd come back to her. She clung to him, returning his kiss with every ounce of love permeating her soul. At the same time she felt her way along their mating bond, all the particles of her being yearning for connection with him. And somehow, he was there, reaching out, linking with her. She imaged a baby. He gasped, his hold on her still deliciously firm, but gentling.

They drew back, eying each other with untrammelled delight, then Lyssica heard her name called. She turned her head; knowing she wore an uncontrollable grin. Her parents grinned back, thrilled by her happiness. Emryn's family stared with various expressions of pleasure or surprise. The elder Fae-male pulled his earlobe.

"Well, Emryn, you told me, but until this moment I didn't believe; there's definitely a mate bond between you and your lady. It's very pleasing." He cast a glance at Duke Yanvian. "You and I have much to discuss, Yanvian."

Her father nodded. "I agree, Bregal."

Lyssica pointed at Emryn's father. "You also need to talk with me, Alpha Kynth-Papan. I'm Emryn's mate just as much as he's my consort, and I speak for myself."

Bregal cocked his head. "Ah, my new daughter is an Alpha too. That's brilliant. It means Emryn's pack tether can be adapted."

Lyssica narrowed her eyes. "Moved to me?"

"Yes, but not totally. A pack of two or three isn't enough for a healthy balance, so a minor link to the Destrion Changeling Clan must continue." Bregal rubbed his chin. "But your relationship provides enough stability for visits to be by choice and not because Emryn is forced to recharge his connection." Joy surged along the bond from Emryn to Lyssica and back again; the last hurdle in their relationship had been overcome.

"Wonderful!"

Bregal nodded and turned in Treymeron's direction. "Didn't catch your name during the earlier introductions, young lordling."

He took the hint. "Treymeron Aphiski, at your service, Kynth-lord Bregal."

Bregal nodded. "Well, I need to correct you on something you said about ... "

Emryn flung up a hand, interrupting. "Thank you Papan, but I believe it's my news to share."

"Sorry, son." His father smiled sheepishly.

"News?" Treymeron's eyebrows elevated.

Emryn met his gaze. "Yes, news." He swallowed, glanced at Lyssica in his arms. "You got one thing wrong, Trey. Lyssica *is* expecting our baby. She just told me.

A look of scepticism flashed across Treymeron's face. "She told you? When you've either been fused at the lips or talking with us the whole time?"

Emryn grinned. "Communication takes many forms, Trey. She definitely told me. Plus, I both sense and scent the changes in her."

Staring in chagrin, Treymeron thrust hands to hips. "Holy snapping swamp turtles! Another one? I can't believe it! What is with all this fertility going around? Can't anyone keep it in their pants?"

Duke Yanvian laughed. "Maybe it's catching?"

A look of horror crossed Treymeron's face. His hands came up to form an ancient sign of warding and turning, he bolted through a side door. As it slammed shut behind him, Lyssica nestled into Emryn's arms.

"Thank you for honouring your vows to me, Emryn."

His smile was tender. "I always will, my darling. I have your name engraved on my heart. From now until forever, it's you and me."

"Oh, Emryn, I love you." More than content, Lyssica sighed and cuddled deeper into the arms of her mate.

The End

~ THE END ~

Thank you for reading Lyssica and Emryn's story. I hope you enjoyed it. If you'd like to find out what happens next, then I recommend Treymeron and Athys' story!

Find it here:
Mistletoe and Meddling

ACKNOWLEDGMENTS

Thank you to:
1. My imagination for getting me started
2. My daughter, Samantha, for believing in me and for kicking me in the butt when I doubted myself
3. Fellow APP anthology members: Leisl, Marnie and Samantha for their expertise, advice and constant encouragement
4. My furry girl, Lexie, for all her cuddles
5. Ice cream and tea, for always being available …

GLOSSARY

Main Characters in this story:

- Lady Lyssica Aphiski – Fae-lady from the Papillion family of the Lepidopter-fae
- Kynthlord Emryn Arion Phengaris – a beta of the Destrion Kynthcat changeling Clan.

Lyssica's Parents:

- Duke Papillion – Yanvian Cosmo Aphiski
- Duchesse Papillion -Azura Gracilla Neptulide Aphiski

Her siblings in birth order:

- DeMaksim Yanvian Aphiski (Hero of Book 2: 'Ancestors and Expectations'.)
- Lyssica Fern Aphiski (Heroine of Book 3: 'Blizzards and Beginnings'.)
- Janeska Lyria Aphiski – twin to Tindresse
- Tindresse Azura Aphiski – twin to Janeska
- Treymeron Cosmo Aphiski
- Armelle Gracilla Aphiski
- Zhulija Juniper Aphiski

Sibling mates:

- Dario Calaspon Eribifax a.k.a. The Unseelie Beast; Hero of Book 1: 'Filigree and Fate'; Zhulija's mate/consort

- Cherith Vanitheriel Beriaden (half Undine-Fae/half Eldwytch-Fae) and one of triplets; Heroine of Book 2: Ancestors and Expectations; DeMaksim's mate/consort.

Emryn's Parents:

- Kynth-lord and Clan Alpha Bregal Fangorn Phengaris
- Kynth-lady Renfa Urlnyth-Phengaris

Emryn's siblings:

- Delano Tarhee Phengaris – brother
- Tucker Rory Phengaris – brother

The Fae Queens, cousins who'd decided to unite the Queendom and rule jointly:

- Seelie Queen Dianathke Morgana (Castle Elrodel)
- Unseelie Queen Maerovana Titania (Castle Synternesse)

Random characters:

- Antigony Lyonetti – Lyssica's personal assistant
- Bardia – gate guard at the Papillion estate
- Brandon – coach driver from Garadenya Fortress/Duchy
- Britha – Captain of guard at Garadenya Fortress/Duchy.
- Brom – guard at Papillion estate
- Countess of Cossidae
- Cyrano – guard at Garadenya Fortress/Duchy
- Jarith – guard at Garadenya Fortress /Duchy
- Lorth Entanglit – Major-domo at Papillion estate

- Lozito – gate guard at Papillion
- Minksalt – Major domo at Garadenya Fortress/Duchy
- Naseem – guard at Garadenya Fortress/Duchy
- Vingle – guard at Garadenya Fortress/Duchy
- Vinny – stable youth at Papillion
- Vystan – guard at Papillion estate

The Visiting Tri-moon Folk at Papillion Estate:

- Lady Kerrigold Anaya Helioden
- Lord Melkaz Brayg Eriocraan
- Lord Perris Haragen Momphiday
- Lord Roland Jarn Arrelgyre.
- Lord Tanjil Rosset Blastobarm
- Lord Venaday Quartz Tortrician

Note:

This series is Speculative and based in Faery. The family around whom the stories are based are Lepidopter-fae: that is Fae-folk with butterfly/moth wings. Other Fae races also appear. So far in my series, these include:

- Dracons,
- Undine water-fae,
- Trolls,
- Redcap goblins,
- Eldwytch mages,
- Shapeshifters – in this story they're Kynthcats: a large, lion-like cat with a mocha coat, a chocolate mane, pale glowing eyes, gnarled, curving horns (like a goat) and a whip like tail.
- Shapeshifter Sand Seers – folk of the Changeling clans who practice divination
- Vart-demons – a type of demon

Various animals including some I have invented for my own purposes, including:

- Wood bunnies – as opposed to just bunnies or rabbits, an Easter connection of sorts
- Blush cheeked chirpers – little birds
- Devil-rabbit – an evil rabbit, minion of The Bodach
- Kynthcat – See shapeshifters
- Duskit – a purple blue multi coloured little creature. Cross between a kitten, a squirrel and a possum.
- Pinkerpush – Treymeron's duskit
- Dash, Splash and Crash – Yanvian's duskits.
- Vulpiawolf- a type of wolf with a spiky rough body pelt, legs without fur and a spiked tail tip. They're greenish grey in colour and smell like wet fur.

There are also appearances by Goddesses, Gods and their consorts:

- Ostara – also known as Eostre – Unseelie Goddess of Spring, fertility and new beginnings, renewal and rebirth. She represents the Spring Equinox, when night and day are of equal length, which in this story I've labelled Ostara Day. Her symbols are the hare, the egg, all Spring flowers, dragons/serpents, a Celtic cross in a circle and the colours of bright green, gold and purple.
- Olwen – Seelie Goddess of Sunlight and Spring
- Modron – Autumn Goddess
- The Cailleach (pronounced Kellyark) Goddess of the cold and winds. Also called The Veiled One and The Queen of Winter. A crone for half the year and young for the six months after Winter's end.
- The Bodach (pronounced bowdark) consort of Cailleach, a mischievous prankster, not always pleasant.

Often appears as an old man dressed in poor farming clothes, chewing a straw, with an old hat perched low on his head.

IF YOU LOVED THIS ONE...

Please leave a review!

Reviews really help authors; it directs our books into the right kind of hands, which in turn allows me to keep writing more books for you to enjoy.

So, if you had a blast reading this story, I'd be ever so grateful if you left a review wherever you can.

Thank you!

Can new love eclipse old fears?

When Lord Treymeron Aphiski arrives at the Palace of Elrodel for his Tri-moon apprenticeship, he's hoping for a fresh start - but never in his wildest dreams did he imagine he'd be made assistant to Queen Dianathke's chief advisor.

Lord Athys Castniidae, Earl of Rengarth is not only capable, kind and generous, he's also incredibly handsome and has a lovely sister to boot. Inca is every bit as witty and intelligent as her brother, and together they mentor Trey in his first assignment; planning the palace's Yule solstice celebrations.

The festivities are threatened when an unknown creature attacks the palace, forcing Trey, Athys and Inca to sideline their preparations to investigate the mystery. But Trey's confusing attraction to both Athys and Inca continues to grow until the truth is revealed, forcing them to either make a stand or lose everything they've struggled to achieve.

Too bad Trey's spent his entire life hiding from the spotlight, Athys is keeping secrets and Inca … well. Be careful what you wish for this Yule, because you just might get it.

~

Read on for a sneak preview of Chapter One!

CHAPTER ONE

TREYMERON

Thrap, thrap, thrap.

Treymeron Aphiski glared at the door, offended by the interruption to his quiet time. Of all the skills he possessed, why couldn't seeing through an opaque piece of wood be one of them? He still wasn't certain agreeing to participate in the Tri-moon training program at the Palace of Elrodel had been the best idea, but it was too late to back out now. Plus, his goal of finding a life and a career somewhere other than home at the Papillion duchy could only happen if he left that home. But the palace was huge, bigger than his expectations and it made him uneasy.

Frowning, he scanned his messy room, then shrugged and grabbed the jerkin he'd tossed over a chair. Dodging haphazardly placed furniture and open boxes, he struggled into his tunic as he crossed the room. He eased the door open a handspan and peered out. The opposite grey stone wall of the hallway was all he could see through the narrow opening, then a movement down low caught his eye.

Marda, the house brownie, touched her forelock. "Sorry to bother you, Lord Treymeron, but this here is Athys Castniidae,

Earl of Rengarth. He said you'd be expecting him." She gestured at someone he couldn't see, then a tall, smiling Fae-male stepped around Marda, peering back at Trey through the narrow gap.

Wow.

His tongue clove to the roof of his mouth as he clutched the edges of the door in frozen befuddlement and stared at this very tall friend of his brother-in-law Dario.

Whose smile was the stuff of dreams.

And aimed at him.

Open-mouthed, unable to look away, Trey simply blinked while the brownie's words of introduction seeped into his skull, then drifted away like thistledown. His Adam's apple bobbed on a hard swallow. He realised, for the first time ever, he was suffering no discomfort in holding the gaze of someone who wasn't a parent or a sibling. This was a stranger. One whose gaze skewered him, yet offered warm recognition as well.

He should look away, because staring like this was surely rude, but he couldn't. Why couldn't he sever the connection? But, how could he – anyone – look away from this astonishing vision of masculine magnificence?

Accented by a single beaded braid caressing the right side of his face, glittering blonde hair swept across Athys' aristocratic forehead and haloed his head, neck and shoulders in lustrous splendour. Teal eyes glowed with a gilded radiance belied by the faintly knit brows in his long, narrow, creamy-gold face. Add in a blade of a nose, high cheekbones, well-shaped lips above a smooth, firm chin, and Trey stood shivering. He clamped the door between desperate fingers; Athys was an entrancing Golden God and he wanted to lick the handsome warrior anywhere he could.

That was when Trey's mouth ran away with him. "You're Athys? Are you sure? Because I was told Athys was away until tomorrow and it's not tomorrow yet."

The corners of Athys' beautiful lips ticked up in a smile, while Trey continued to gawp like a landed fish, mentally kicking himself for the foolishness of his words. When would he learn to put his brain in gear before he opened his mouth?

The Golden God's voice was as deep and sinfully delicious as the rest of him. "I'm definitely Athys and I'm back a day early." The deep timbre invaded the narrow gap between them like Trey's favourite sweet and creamy cheese-filled pastry, wrapping him in scrumptious yumminess. "I thought we could chat and get acquainted before the official Tri-moon program gets underway in the morning. Does that work for you, Treymeron?"

Eyes drifting shut, Trey basked in warm sensations, as they seeped through the pores of his skin; deeper and deeper, until the beautiful tendrils wrapped and stroked his parched soul. It was blissful. He wanted more. In fact, his inclinations were pushing him to climb Athys as if he were a tree, then cling tight and, and ...

And that was no sane way to think about the Fae-male with whom Dario had arranged Trey's Tri-moon stay. He swept his tongue across his lips; was there a drugging scent in the air here? Some sort of craziness induced by pollen?

"Treymeron? Hello? May I come in and speak with you?"

The warm honeyed strands were still cuddling him, but oh! Words, issuing from the Golden God's attractive mouth, suddenly registered in his loopy mind; his eyes shot open on a gasp. "Holy snapping swamp turtles! So sorry, your lordship. I don't know what came over me. Of course you may, but how is it that you're here? I mean, it's not that you aren't wanted; you're more than welcome." He jerked the door wide, a flush scalding his face. Heaving in a breath, he fought for serenity and control. Athys was high in the Queens' regard. Wouldn't it be wonderful to be in such a valued position? To know where you fit in the world?

Athys smiled. "Thank you, Treymeron."

As he moved aside, the suite's disorganised chaos was revealed and Marda's hands flew to her cheeks. "My Lord Treymeron! What have you done to your room? It was so neat, so well-prepared, and now look!"

Peering around, Trey swallowed. "I'm sorry but I wasn't

comfortable." He threw her a challenging stare. "You said I could make myself at home."

The brownie threw her hands in the air. "But there's furniture and cushions everywhere!"

Athys glanced into the room; there was no doubt he was taking note of the mess.

Trey bit his lip. "I haven't finished." He smoothed a hand down his rumpled jerkin. "If you'd returned tomorrow, like you said, this would've been neat and tidy once more."

Now Marda's hands were clasped at her bosom. "But you're changing everything!"

He winced. "I know, but if this is my room and I'm to live here for the next few months, I need to have things organised in a way that doesn't make my neck crawl."

Athys bit his lower lip, but nodded gravely. "Understandable. That sensation is never a welcome one."

The little brownie was peering around. "Where are the flowers I specially picked?"

Trey flushed. "I know you went to a lot of trouble and I really appreciate it, but ..." He bit his lip. "I'm sorry, they stunk the room up, so I threw them out the window."

Her face screwed up. "The brithaglio lace doilies?"

He tilted his head, pointed to one side of the room. "Stuffed in a closet."

"And the antique bronze figurine crafted by the famous Farrugio?"

His hands went to his hips. "That disgusting satyr leering over the terrified nymph? So hideously unpleasant! I can't get over how ugly it is! I had to embalm it in those lace thingies before I shoved it in the back of the closet and covered it with other stuff. It gives me the heebie jeebies! That Furruglio guy must have been some kind of pervert!" He trailed off at the expression of horror on the brownie's face and clapped a hand over his mouth as he took a step back.

A snort came from Athys but Marda let out such an outraged

howl, it caused a painful ringing in Trey's ears. Shaking his head, he retreated further, only stopping when something hard clipped the back of his calves and threw him off balance.

"Oh shite!" Arms windmilling, he toppled, rear end forcefully meeting the sharp edge of the box he'd backed into, before he bounced sideways and down, to where the solid floor awaited. The momentum flattened his upper body, forcing his feet and legs high into the air. For a moment he feared a somersault was inevitable – but then he rocked forward and his feet slammed back to the floor. Pain filled him and he groaned. Miserably aware of the flush rising from his chest, flowing inexorably up his neck, spreading until it swamped his cheeks with glowing humiliation, he sagged. Was it possible the floor could crack open, let him fall through, then snap shut again?

A scream rent the air. Probably Marda. Through his agonised daze, he was vaguely aware of Athys shoving the door wide and striding in.

The beautiful Golden God dropped to his knees and leaned over Trey's supine body. "Treymeron! Look at me!"

Forcing his eyes to meet Athys' worried gaze, Trey was vaguely aware of Marda wailing about the disordered state of his rooms, but who could care about that with this adorable Fae-male looming over him? What was pain when beautiful hair fell forward to cocoon them in a shiny curtain? When those enticing lips shaped words …

Which dropped like stones. "Marda, please stop! They're only things. If you like them so much, put them in your own room."

The harsh order jolted Trey out of his haze. He focused on Athys' concerned face, now filling his field of vision.

"Shite, Treymeron! Are you hurt?" Large warm hands slid down his arms, ran over his body, his legs and back up his torso, finally cupping either side of his jaw. "Tell me where the pain is."

Trey grimaced weakly. "I was *trying* to make a good impression." He huffed a weak chuckle, his eyes falling away. "Waste of time. Oh well – I'll definitely have bruises, just as my pride does.

But you know what they say: 'Pride goeth before a fall.' Or before a bumble foot, tangoing with randomly scattered boxes. Can you tango with boxes? Who would lead as you slide across the floor? The floor! Is it damaged? If it's scraped, I'm happy to work off any repairs. I'm—"

"Very talkative." The hands on his jaw gently raised his face until he again met the crystal blue eyes inspecting him with focused concern. "You didn't appear to hit your head, so you're not dazed. Which means …"

They were interrupted by a litany of 'squees', which accompanied the skittering gallop of little paws crossing the room.

Athys tensed, spinning to face the threat. His hand flew to a sheathed knife at one hip. His nearest leg maintained a kneeling position, but the other leg was suddenly drawn up beneath him, weight on the ball of the foot. "What's this?"

"Oh, that's my Pinkerpush." The tiny duskit raced to Treymeron, trembling as she scaled him to snuggle under his chin. He cooed, raising his arms to cradle her and smoothed his jaw over the softness of her downy head.

Reaching out slowly Athys stroked Pinkerpush's ear. "A duskit. I'm impressed." His fingers dropped so Pinkerpush could sniff them. Trey watched as Pinkie stared up at Athys; her deep blue eyes blinking from a face covered in bright purple fur, before her soft wet nose snuffled his fingers - folk were always fascinated by Pinkerpush. Athys was approved with the swipe of a tiny tongue. Shifting his finger to caress the satiny cheek, he grinned as he refocused on Treymeron. "I see Pinkerpush is quite young; how long have you had her?"

A wobbly smile bloomed. "Pinkerpush was orphaned last winter in a Vulpiawolf attack. I was caring for her and then she wouldn't leave."

"She must feel safe with you."

Trey nodded. "I hope so. I've grown to love her and I'd be lost if she left now."

Athys nodded. "That's understandable." He studied Trey's face intently. "Now, where do you hurt? Any areas of sharp pain?"

Trey's hands fluttered weakly. "No, I'm okay. Oh, wait, my bum aches."

"Hmm. Well you did hit the floor with a wallop, so that wouldn't surprise me." Athys continued to scan him. "Fortunately, I didn't feel any obvious broken limbs or sprains, and nothing looks odd. Are you okay to get up, Treymeron? Here, let me help you."

Trey's eyes drifted shut. "I'm alright and just call me Trey. I'll get up momentarily. Ohh!" A shoulder under his armpit hoisted him like a baby. "How'd you do that? You're a big guy, but I'm no weanling."

Athys chuckled as he gently lowered Treymeron to sit on one of the rearranged dining chairs. "One of my many talents."

Marda appeared next to them, wringing her tiny hands. "Do my lords need assistance? A healer perhaps?"

Trey shook his head. "No, no. Thanks anyway, Marda. Really, it was just a trifling thing. Nothing exciting, or serious like an earthquake—"

A dull roar vibrated the entire building, sending objects rattling and floors, doors and walls moving in a series of waves. The magical colour plumsplat radiated through the ether in frantically shooting sparks.

The chair tipped enough to send Trey sliding into Athys, while Pinkerpush went flying. They crashed to the floor in a twisted heap. Trey found himself lying half on, half off of a very broad chest, legs intertwined, and his face buried in the side of a warm neck. Both of Athys' arms banded tightly around a shaking Trey, then Pinkerpush tried to burrow between them, chittering furiously.

"What in thunder just happened?" Trey could only mumble as he forced himself to breathe, in and out, in and out … The scent of Athys filled his nostrils, a delightful aroma of cinnamon and rose-musk. The movement of his mouth as he spoke pressed his lips into Athys' skin. "Ooh, sorry! I'm not kissing you, although it probably seems like it. But a kiss would be more forceful, done with intent and ... Icklegolia! Me and my silly mouth!" Beneath him, Athys started to shake and his mirth burst from him in a loud chuckle. Trey pulled slowly away, forced his aching body into a sitting position, his skin burning as a blush crept up his features. Squeeing again, Pinkerpush crawled into his lap.

Marda was staring at him with fearful awe. "I d-don't care about the room changes, Lord Treymeron, I really don't! You-you caused an earthquake. That's powerful magic. Please say you weren't angry with anything I said or did!"

"No! No! That wasn't me!" Panic welling, Trey flapped his hands wildly and Pinkerpush's claws gripped his jerkin as he let her go. "I can't ... I didn't ... I wouldn't ..." His voice grew louder with every word.

Large hands clasped his. "Ssh, I've got you." Athys pulled him closer. "Marda, that wasn't Trey."

Marda didn't look convinced. "But he said ... he said the word, then it happened." She pointed at Pinkerpush. "And he's got a familiar."

Trey gasped. "A familiar? Pinkie? No!" He bit his lip. "No, she's my fosterling and my friend, but not my familiar."

"Although, I can see why you might think so, Marda." Athys nodded, one arm cupping Trey's trembling shoulders. "But that was no earthquake. If you look around, you'll see there's no real damage other than a few small things falling over."

Marda frowned. "But there was noise and shaking and magic – I saw plumsplat sparking."

"You're right about that, Marda. It was magic." Athys rubbed Trey's upper back. "But it was portal magic. Very badly constructed portal magic, too, which is why it resembled an earthquake."

"It felt wrong." Trey wearily scrubbed one cheek. "The magic was off."

Athys' mouth thinned. "The magic was 'off', as you put it,

because whoever tried to cast the spell didn't know what they were doing."

Trey's brows furrowed. "How do you know that?"

Athys' lips twisted. "Because I've been present when Queen Dianathke does portal magic and it's nothing like that."

OTHER TALES BY HELLUCY HOWE

~

The Fae Courts

A sweeping fantasy romance series filled with fae, gods, magic… and plenty of adventure!

A Perfectly Paranormal Anthologies

A collection of paranormal romance anthologies in conjunction with several other wonderful authors.

~

To find out more about any of these, visit my website:

www.hellucywrites.com

PART OF THE TRIBE

I love to hear from, and keep in touch with, fellow book worms! If you'd like to spend a little more time together, you can find me in the following places:

FACEBOOK

- A Perfectly Paranormal Anthologies Reader Group - Perfectly Paranormal Paramours

~

Or send me an email at - hellucywrites@gmail.com - I love hearing from readers and authors alike!

ABOUT THE AUTHOR

Meet Hellucy Howe, a Book Dragon who teethed on romantic fairy tales and went on to voraciously devour anything paranormal. Writing was also second nature but became something to do in secret when the stories of her young child mind were ridiculed. Homes were populated with books and hidden caches of story notebooks inspired by a fertile brain and a massive creative streak.

She became a Professional Reader and a Closet Scribbler, convinced no one would want to look at the mad ramblings of someone who hates getting dirt under her fingernails and knows ironing was invented as a torture method.

Nowadays, Helen loves inventing paranormal and fantasy romance from the comfort of her cosy study with a hot cup of tea beside her laptop and her little spaniel, Lexie, snoring at her feet. With her anthology contribution of 'Filigree and Fate', Helen has been dragged kicking and screaming from her closet, into the deer-in-headlights world of being a Real Author.

www.ingramcontent.com/pod-product-compliance
Lightning Source LLC
Chambersburg PA
CBHW020008140726
47904CB00018B/2122